To:

Carrie ♡

From:

Christina

# The Girls of Cornelius Academy

Christina

authorHOUSE®

*AuthorHouse™*
*1663 Liberty Drive, Suite 200*
*Bloomington, IN 47403*
*www.authorhouse.com*
*Phone: 1-800-839-8640*

*First published by AuthorHouse 10/3/2008*

*ISBN: 978-1-4343-1894-7 (sc)*

*Library of Congress Control Number: 2007905867*

*Printed in the United States of America
Bloomington, Indiana*

*This book is printed on acid-free paper.*

## My Acknowledgements

I would like to dedicate this book to my parents, James K. Mensah and Tina Brew-Mensah; and my friends Ariana, Clare, Megan, Jaleelah, Shakira, Carrie, Kelly, Nicole, Jessica K., Jessica P., Allyson, Ryann, Jessica Karpovich, Emily D., Emily M., Emily B., Dana, Allison L., Michelle D., Rachel S., Rachel Z., Jessica C., Jordan, Michael (Richard), David W., Leah, Erin, and Aferba.

Thanks also to AuthorHouse, my entire family (I love you all!), and everyone else who believed in me. *Amy*

I hope you guys enjoy it! This one is for you!

# 1

"Good morning, Mavis Gardens!" The radio broadcaster announced. "It's a beautiful day to get out and—" Larissa sleepily shut off her pink alarm clock and arose from her cashmere blanket she had bought in London. She rubbed the sleep from her eyes before checking the time. Her clock read seven o' clock. As she lifted her head, she felt dizzy, and her head suddenly became too heavy for comfort. And to make matters worse, her Yorkshire terrier puppy dog, Tootsie, jumped onto her belly, using her big, brown eyes to persuade Larissa into petting her. "Not now, Tootsie," she moaned. She lightly pushed her dog away, forcing her onto the ground. Tootsie whined and padded back to her doggie bed with her head bent low.

Larissa did feel bad about treating her dog that way, but she was in such an awful mood, she didn't have enough energy to even care. *This is all Cher's fault,* thought Larissa. And it basically was. If it wasn't for Cher's burning desire to go to a huge end-of-the-summer bonfire just to show everyone she could get into a college party, Larissa would've had an adequate amount of sleep to function properly for the rest of the day.

But she had to admit the party was fun.

Everyone got loose, trying to enjoy every last ounce of summer fun before it was back to a world filled with textbooks and mean teachers. She remembered seeing people dancing crazily on top of their BMW's and Lexus's and chugging down cups after cups filled with Smirnoff Ice. Then after a moment of reminiscing about what had to be one of the wildest parties she had ever been to, she also remembered the worst thing ever done to her.

********

"No," Larissa yelled into her cordless phone. It was after eleven Sunday night, and Cher and Larissa were supposed to be going over their outfits for tomorrow—seeing it was the first day back to school—but instead, Cher was literally pleading with her to attend this stupid bonfire with her.

"But why, Larissa," pouted Cher. "I can't go alone! That would make me look stupid!" Because of her high rank in society, Cher always had to comport herself with elegance and class.

"You're the one who wants to go!" Larissa wanted to say, but wouldn't dare mimic Cher like that.

Instead, she told her, "But I can't go," said Larissa. "You know my mom: she'll start asking me all these questions if she catches me!"

"Then don't get caught!"

"And how do you expect me to do that when they're right downstairs!" Larissa knew her mom and dad were down there having their usual cup of tea, talking about their day, before heading upstairs to their master suite to rest.

"Ugh! Must I think of everything for you?" Cher paused. "Listen. If you can't sneak out of your own house, then why don't you make up some white lie to tell them?"

"What would I say?" She did have an idea of what to say, but she was really just hoping to get out of this situation.

"Be like, *mom, I left my Prada scarf at Cher's and I really need it back. Can I go get it before it gets too late?* You drive down to my pad, pick me up, and we'll go together. All set!"

"Are you even listening to yourself? What parent in their right mind would allow their child to go out this late the night before school just to pick up a stupid scarf? And besides, I don't own Prada scarves!"

"Then what do you suggest?" Larissa could almost guess Cher was rolling her eyes on the other side of the phone.

Larissa paused for a moment. "Well––I was thinking I could not go?"

"Fine, don't go. I'll just tell everyone you peed yourself when you were talking to the cute guy that works at Saks!"

Larissa had a crush on the guy Cher was referring to. She didn't really know his name, but with his hazel eyes and dimply smile, who cared! He was adorable and that's all that mattered. She never peed herself though.

Her mouth hung open. "Cher, you wouldn't do that to me, would you?"

"Never said I couldn't…"

"I can't believe this," Larissa grumbled to herself. She looked outside her floor-length window that overlooked the pristine beach just a quarter of a mile away from her large estate, not sure where to look next. The ocean waves swept across the pearl-white beach as peaceful as anything. *Oh how I wish I could be as 'at peace' like the ocean.*

"Tick, tock, tick, tock. So, what's gonna be? Are you in, or are you out?"

Larissa didn't answer because she was lost in thought. *But then again, everyone at school, including Cher, brag on and on about how they snuck out to go to some frat party and hooked up someone. It seems like they have a lot of fun…and seeing this is technically the last day of summer…*

"You owe me," mumbled Larissa.

"Does this mean you'll come?"

Larissa bit her lower lip. "Yeah," she sighed.

Cher squealed so loudly into the phone, Larissa swore even the residents of Washington State heard. "I am so glad we're going to this! Everyone will be so jealous!"

"Whatever." Unlike Cher, Larissa didn't indulge herself in making her peers envy her extravagant lifestyle.

"Now let's talk clothes." Larissa heard Cher moving about in her large bedroom towards her equally huge walk-in closet. "What are you going to wear," she asked after a while.

"Something clean," Larissa arrogantly answered. She wasn't in the mood to go crazy over clothes like she normally did, especially for an event she was being forced to go to.

"Cut the sarcasm, Larissa. I mean, what do you want to wear *besides* something clean?"

"Well, what else do you want me to say? I haven't exactly had enough time to think about an outfit idea."

"Maybe I can help." Cher was silent for a moment.

"No, it's alright," she murmured, "I can find something on my own!"

By now, Cher was starting to get the hint that maybe going to this party wasn't something Larissa wanted to do after all. Maybe she was going for her? "What's wrong," she asked, "aren't you happy you're going to the biggest party of your life?"

"Sure I am!" Larissa pulled her hair back into a ponytail with a hair tie she had wrapped around her wrist. "I'm just a little tired, that's all."

"Are you sure?"

"Positive."

"In that case, wake up! I need your help picking out an outfit, ASAP! If I'm going to get a cute college guy's number, I must look, at least, like a Tyra Banks knock-off!"

Larissa pretended to yawn and said, "Okay."

At that point, Cher kept mumbling to herself, rejecting the bathing suits or cover-ups she described over the phone. After a long five minutes of picking and *not* choosing, Cher settled on a white Juicy Couture string bikini and its matching tube dress. Then she began raving about how great the party would be and how her hot choices would get her in instantly with the college guys that would be roaming around. Blah, blah, blah!

Finally around ten fifteen, after at least an hour of nonstop I-can't-wait-to-see-the-look-on-all-the-girls-faces-at-school-when-we-tell-them-we-went-to-an-actual-college-party speech from Cher, Larissa slipped out of bed, tiptoed over to her walk-in closet, and then, in a swift motion, peeled off her cotton pajamas and slipped into a simple cream-colored Milly bikini, a Trina Turk sundress and a pair of sandals. At her vanity, she coated her eyelashes with waterproof mascara and smeared a very sheer lip shine on her lips.

Once she was sure every inch of her appearance was flawless—flawless enough to snag a man that Cher wouldn't steal—she grabbed her Burberry handbag, stuffed with the usual: car keys to her Maserati, cell phone, compact, a tube of lip gloss and waterproof mascara just in case of retouches, as well as a breath mint, just in case. *Now how do I sneak out of here without being detected?* With Cher talking endlessly, she never even got the chance to ask Cher how to break out. First thing: she had to leave her room.

The upstairs hallway was filled with the aroma of vanilla-scented candles from Pier 1 Imports. The orange-yellowish glow gave the space an ominous, yet calming feel. *Maybe I can try the Service Door,* Larissa suggested to herself. All the maids would be up in their quarters by now, so there was no way she could get caught. Without hesitating, Larissa swiftly raced down the back steps––the steps designated for the house help only––and before she could make her escape, she found her driver, Samson sitting at the kitchenette, reading the daily newspaper.

"Hello," he greeted her in his thick British accent. Larissa could sense he was a bit confused. "Is there a reason you are here so late?"

"Uh––" Suddenly, her mind drew a blank. "I was only going––out for some fresh air." When she tried to grab the doorknob, Samson beat her to it.

"Now, now, Ms. Evans, there is no need to lie." He stood up tall and firm then asked, "Where are you going? The truth this time."

Larissa knew Sam wouldn't let her go that easy. He had caught her, and there was no way around it. "Please don't tell mom and dad. I'll be back soon, honest."

He leaned forward and kissed Larissa's pale, blonde hair. "I'll cover for you this time, but please do be careful."

A wide smile spread across her clear face. Sometimes, she loved having such a cool driver. Normally, he didn't rat on Larissa when it came to these kinds of things. "Thanks. I owe you big time!" As she was walking out the door, she heard Sam say:

"Now don't come home drunk, you hear?"

Larissa answered, "yes, sir," and shut the door behind her.

********

The party was already kicking into high gear by the time the girls got there. They were greeted by, maybe twenty people or so, dancing suggestively to a pop number on the asphalt parking lot, holding red plastic cups filled with beer.

"Ah! I'm so excited!" Cher squealed as Larissa maneuvered her car into an empty parking space that wasn't occupied with lounging college kids. The two stepped out and met up with their friends, Carlos, Tommy, Mitchell, and T. J, who were sitting on the truck bed of Tommy's black Escalade truck.

"Looking good, boys," Cher commented teasingly. She loved messing with guys' hearts like that.

"You're not looking so bad either," Mitchell flirted back.

Cher couldn't help but giggle.

"So what did we miss," Larissa asked, veering off subject.

"Nothin' much," T.J took a drag from his Camel Lite cigarette. He had started smoking as a way to relieve his depression after breaking up with his girlfriend, Hannah. "All we've really done is smoke, drink booze, dance, oh, and I think they were doing some weenie roasting earlier."

"Gross," exclaimed Cher, pretending to gag herself. She hated to eat fattening food like that. For some reason, it made her sick to her stomach to even think about it. "All in favor for some lobster bisque, say I."

"I," said the guys, raising their pointer fingers high.

"What's so bad about weenies," asked Larissa.

Cher let out a snort. "For one thing, the name is even disgusting. It makes me think of––" But before she could finish her statement, she was interrupted by a random voice.

"Hey, guys," the voice said. It was Jennifer Lockbourne. She went to Cornelius Academy, just like Cher and her friends. Cher had met her last summer at the local country club after they played a game of tennis together.

"Jenny," Cher asked, "what are you doing here?" She was a bit disappointed she wouldn't be able to rub this event in her face.

"My sister, Lauren"––she pointed at a blonde haired lady standing around with a couple of guys and girls, chatting closer to the shore––"is friends with the guy throwing the party, and I decided to come with."

This made Cher even more envious that Jenny had connections with college students already. She hated it when people had more than she had, even though that was quite rare. "Whatever. Anyway, what have you been up to since you've been here?"

Larissa jumped in. "See any cute guys yet?"

Cher's stomach churned at the thought of Jenny getting in contact with the guys before she even had a chance to settle in.

Jenny giggled, "no, not yet. But I'm still on the lookout!"

Cher let out a sigh of relief when no one was looking.

Mitchell rolled his eyes. "You girls are all the same. Why would you obsess over other guys," he pointed at his crew, "when you have us!"

"No offense, Mitch, but you're just not my taste," Cher bluntly answered. And with that, the girls left them, laughing the entire way to the sandy coast.

But as soon as Larissa touched the sand, she stopped short in her tracks while Cher and Jenny went ahead, not even realizing Larissa wasn't with them anymore. The guy that seemed to have taken her breath away was about six foot five and had shaggy blonde hair, a cute smile, and the most amazing body Larissa had ever had the pleasure of seeing! *It's like the hunk gods have beamed him down to me!* Larissa thought entranced by his looks.

She so desperately wanted to go over there and talk to him, just to know the man behind those sapphire eyes, but the chance of him even paying her any mind was slim. And besides, what if he didn't find her attractive at all? What if he thought she was some loser high school kid, who thinks she's cool just because she's at a college party and drinking tons of alcohol without her parents ever finding out! *I bet the girls he's into are more sophisticated than I am, and prettier, and take tough courses like trig or physics!* She couldn't go over there.

As she was walking over to her friends, who were now chatting it up with a couple of guys both wearing board shorts and T-shirts, a football came flying across the dark, star-filled sky and landed right in front of her. She picked it up and searched for the owner of the ball when she discovered it belonged to The Guy.

"Hey, over here," he called out to her.

Larissa did the best she could to throw it back. The Guy caught it, but instead of going back to his game with his friends, he ran towards her.

"Lance, what are you doing?" his curly-haired friend yelled.

"I'll be back." He reached Larissa and quickly ran his fingers through his hair.

Larissa couldn't believe he was standing only two feet away from her, practically breathing down her neck. "So, your name is Lance," Larissa started. "Cute name."

Lance grinned. He had a chipped tooth that was noticeable, but Larissa didn't seem to mind. "That's what most people call me." He stared directly into her eyes. "Maybe you can tell me what people call you."

"Larissa, Larissa Evans." She left out her middle name 'Kate'. After all, it was her grandmother's name.

Lance held out his hand and shook hers. "Very nice to meet you, Larissa Evans."

Larissa covered her mouth to hide her giggles. "So you're the charmer type, huh?" She stared up into his eyes for a while. "I like that."

They stayed still for what seemed like forever. Larissa didn't make an effort to move. All she wanted was the sweet, salty sea breeze whisk around them and meld their bodies into one. "So where do you go to school?"

She froze. She wasn't sure if she should tell the truth and say she was in high school or not. *But what if he backs off? I don't want him to. I* really *like him!* "Pepperdine," she quickly said.

"Ah, so I'm guessing your dad must be loaded."

"Pretty much, but I got there on scholarship." Larissa was amazed at how easy lying really was. It just seemed to get easier and easier every time…

Lance blushed in embarrassment. "Hey, sorry about that. I just——"

"It's cool. You see, I was in eleventh grade, but I was so smart, they promoted me to college!"

"So do you think you can help me with my homework sometime?"

Larissa inched towards him, giving off the impression she wanted to be kissed. "Maybe when I have some extra time, but, in the mean time, maybe you can help me get to know you better."

He chuckled. "Sure, follow me."

Cher was fishing through the cooler for a drink.

Jenny had gone off to find her sister and talk to her friends. Whatever, Cher said when Jenny left her alone. Even though she was ticked she had to be alone at a party like this, she used this time to scope the area for some hot guys. But before she could begin her search, she needed refreshment quick!

She didn't feel like drinking beer—strict diet, and it tasted nasty! She didn't want to drink any form of alcohol—strict diet, and she was driving herself home. And she didn't want to drink any strong drink after midnight. Good choice.

*Ugh! Hasn't this guy ever heard of mineral water?* Cher rolled her chocolate-colored eyes. *This is exactly why I don't like coming to these cheap bonfire parties! The only reason I came was to meet a hot college guy, make out with him, ask him on a date, and rub it in Larissa's face!*

Cher bitterly grabbed Dasani bottled water and began taking tiny sips as she scoured the large party crowd. Some were dancing—including T. J, Mitchell, and two girls they most likely met—on the parking lot to music blaring out of a Chevrolet's stereo system. Others were still sitting by the bonfire, roasting marshmallows and some hotdogs.

The host was grilling some meat on the portable grill he had brought along. Tommy and Carlos were talking to him as they were drinking something out of plastic red cups. *That'd better not be alcohol, 'cause I'm not driving their sorry butts home!*

Then . . .

*Wait a minute!* Cher watched with hatred as Larissa, the same girl who fought tooth and nail to stay home, flirting with an *extremely* cute college guy! He had his arms wrapped around her as he taught her how to throw a football. Larissa wore his hat proudly.

Cher just couldn't understand it. *How can Larissa, Ms. I-don't-want-to-sneak-out-because-I'm-a-goody-two-shoes, get a Prince Charming like that? Wasn't she the one who didn't want to come?* Cher tucked her short bob of hair ––courtesy of her favorite exclusive salon, Starlet––behind her ear and glared jealously as Larissa continued to flirt.

*Besides, if anyone is getting attention from a college guy, it should be me! I have more experience in dating, whereas Larissa hasn't even been asked out on* one *date!*

The guy leaned over and kissed Larissa softly on her flushed cheek.

At this point, Cher grew enraged. *That's it! I'm stopping this madness even if it* kills *me!* She began to storm over to Larissa and the guy. Along the way, she chucked her bottled water carelessly onto the sand. *Mental note: bring mineral water to the next bonfire you attend.* And with that, she continued her mission . . . and no one could stop her.

Lance had stopped his lesson with Larissa and was now sitting on the sand with her, watching the ocean. Larissa rested her head on his broad shoulder. She had never felt this intimate or confident before in her life. For the first time ever, Larissa was finally the star, and not the one hiding in the shadows.

But not for long.

"Do you think I'll ever be able to see you again," Lance murmured into her ear.

Larissa pulled away from him and stared into his eyes, just to make sure he wasn't joking around. But his blue eyes were firm and filled with seriousness. He really *did* want to see her again! "Well, if you feel we have a chance, why not?"

He grinned. "Great. I'll go get a pen." He leaned over and brushed his lips across hers. "Don't you go anywhere!"

Lance smiled and ran up the shore towards a green Mustang.

"Hey, Larissa!" Cher's booming voice startled her from behind.

Larissa gazed up at her. "What are you doing here?"

"I came with you, remember?" Cher made a place for herself on the sand without being invited. "So, what are you doing, you naughty little girl!"

"Me?" Larissa fidgeted with her fingers. "What are you talking about?"

"Oh don't give me that!" Cher looked over her shoulder at Lance, who was still searching for a pen in his glove compartment. "I mean, what are you doing with that guy?"

"Who, Lance? He's just a guy I met…"

"Just a guy you met?" Cher rolled her eyes. "Larissa, we're not babies anymore, and I can tell when you're interested in someone. So tell me"––she leaned closer to her–"are you interested in him?"

Larissa glanced back at Lance. It looked like he finally found what he was looking for. And she was starting to think the same thing. "Yes! Yes, yes, and a million times yes! He's so dreamy, and romantic, and kind, and––"

"I get it! You don't have to give a frickin' novel!" Cher cursed under her breath. No way could she let this relationship go on. I mean, how would it make her look if Larissa, the *second* most popular girl at school having a hot boyfriend––not to mention a hot *college* boyfriend––and Cher, the supreme ruler over the school, having no one? Not good.

Lance came jogging back to Larissa only to find Cher with her. "Larissa, do you know her?"

"Um––" she stood up, brushing the sand off her butt. "She's my friend, Lance. Cher, meet Lance; Lance, this is Cher."

"Hey."

"Nice to meet you, Lance," Cher greeted. She was about to walk away when she turned back to Larissa. "Oops! I forgot! Larissa, I think Jenny needed you for something."

Larissa raised her eyebrow. "Something like what?"

"Wouldn't say, but I think she's having a 'feminine issue'?"

"Maybe you should go check on her," Lance suggested. "Don't worry, I'll wait."

"Thanks," she grinned.

Cher rolled her eyes in disgust.

Larissa walked up the shore towards the parking lot. This was Cher's cue. And she only had little time to

17

make everything right. "So, where do you go to school," she asked.

"I'm a sophomore at UCLA. I'm on sports scholarship. And you?"

"No kidding! I'm a freshman at Stanford," she lied. "I major in law."

Lance seemed puzzled. "So how do you know Larissa," he inquired. "She told me she goes to Pepperdine."

"Pepperdine," Cher blurted. Suddenly, Cher was starting to realize maybe Larissa wasn't the goody two-shoes she always appeared to be. *I can't believe Larissa would lie like that? And she claimed she couldn't lie! I knew I shouldn't have believed her. Well, I guess I'll just have to teach her a lesson on how lying is wrong!* So Cher did the only logical thing to do. And that was laugh.

"What's so funny," he asked her.

"I can't believe Larissa would lie to you like that," she giggled some more. "And you believed her every word!"

Lance was confused. "What are you talking about? She doesn't even seem like the lying type!"

Cher took a deep breath. "Well, like they say: never judge a book by its cover!"

"Your point?"

"My point is––Larissa's a dropout! She used to go to Pepperdine, but that was before she was caught making out with a professor in her dormitory."

Lance couldn't find the words to speak for a moment. "What do you mean? She's been lying to me the whole time?"

"Duh, that's what she always does! How else do you think she gets young guys like you to sleep with her?"

He paused. "Wait. What do you mean by "young" guys?"

Cher scoffed. "She didn't tell you this either? God, is she a bad girl or what?"

"Would you just get to the point," he spat.

Cher jumped at his sudden rage.

That was when Lance soon breathed deeply and said, "I'm sorry. I'm just upset, that's all."

"Apology accepted. I understand you're angry, but that shouldn't be any reason to get you down, now should it?"

Lance sighed. "You're right. I don't need to lose my cool over her, do I?"

"Absolutely not! Who is Larissa anyway?" Cher inched closer to him. "You see, I feel you deserve better than that whore"––she brushed her finger across the stubble on his chin––"and I'm ready to prove that to you." Then she placed her lips onto his. And Lance didn't try to fight back.

*In your face, Evans!* Cher thought vindictively.

Larissa was stomping back to Lance and Cher. She had just discovered that Jenny didn't even call her. Plus, she figured that out when she saw Jenny was about to leave with Lauren and some other people. Apparently, the party was getting lame, and they were going to chill in a Dairy Queen parking lot, eating Blizzards. *I should've known Cher was lying! She hardly tells the . . .* Then right before her very eyes, she witnessed Cher and Lance kissing passionately underneath the moonlit sky.

"Cher, how could you do this to me," Larissa wailed as she ran over to the kissing couple. Cher and Lance pulled away from each other.

"Now you stand right there, you lying, backstabbing skank!" cried Lance.

Larissa let out a tiny gasp and glared at him with the most fearful look on her face. "Lance? Are you really talking to me that way?"

"Why not? After all, you deserve it."

She pointed at her. "I deserve this kind of treatment?"

"Of course!"

"Why would you say that?"

"Don't act like you don't know," he turned to Cher. "I mean do you do this to all the guys you hang around with––oh, wait, *sleep* with!"

"Lance!"

"Enough," Cher silenced them both. She turned to Lance. "Now you listen to me, you no-good-two-timing-jerk! No one talks to my friend like that!"

"But——"

"Hey! I didn't say you could talk, did I?" Cher pointed her finger straight at him. "You've been warned. Don't you ever, *ever* set foot near us again 'cause if you do, it'll be your last time! You hear me?" Cher turned to Larissa. "Let's bounce."

And that's when they left, never looking back at Lance once.

Now she was lying in her bed, still thinking about last night. It seemed so bizarre to her. One minute he acted like he really liked her; the next he treated her like dirt. *Is that how all college guys act?* But when she thought harder about it, Lance accused her after Cher came by. *Could it be Cher misinformed him about me?* It made perfect sense: Cher admitted she only went to the party to make people jealous, and she felt the only way to do that was get a guy! But since she was mad Larissa got one before her, she decided to take him her way!

She checked her clock again. It read seven fifteen. She stood up, and this time, her head wasn't as heavy. She did have some difficulty walking, but she could manage. Soon her fatigue would wear off as soon as she took a warm shower. Soon, her phone rang. Her caller ID read "Cher".

"Speaking of the devil," Larissa muttered. She slowly pressed the Talk button, hoping she could keep the conversation as minimal as possible.

"What took you so long," Cher demanded.

Larissa opened her mouth to say something, but Cher cut her off.

"Never mind. You're forgiven. Anyway, do you know what day it is?"

Larissa nearly forgot. It was the first day back. Larissa was suddenly feeling dizzy again, and it wasn't because of the lack of sleep. She knew this would just be another long, boring conversation about Cher, and her outfit, and let's not forget, her plan to humiliate the new kids at school. "Hello! Did you hear me?" She literally screamed into the phone.

She snapped out of her dizziness. "Sorry," she said. She stared out the window. "I'm not feeling too well."

"Did you drink too much?"

"No." *Just had my life ruined that's all!*

Cher said nothing for some time. "It's not about that Lance jerk from last night, is it?"

"I'm fine, honest," she answered, clenching her teeth. *She had to bring up Lance!*

"Sure?"

"Definitely," Larissa stood up and paced around her room. "I don't even know why I bothered worrying about him in the first place."

"That's my girl! Anyway, I have the most amazing news to tell you! It's like God has finally answered my prayers."

Larissa rolled her eyes. I don't think *God answers prayers for devils-in-training!* "I'm listening." She kept staring at her painted toenails.

Cher took a deep breath. "So, it was six o' clock in the morning when some chick––I don't know her name–– sent a chain message to me, saying Chris Tyler is officially single!! Can you imagine?"

Chris Tyler was the one of the hottest boys at school. He was African American, just like Cher, and he had very light skin, again, just like Cher. He also had brown eyes and short black hair, and he was an amazing basketball player. He once took the school to the state finals. He wasn't really Larissa's type, so she could care less if he was single or not! But that didn't mean he deserved a conceited braggart like Cher!

"And you actually believe those things," Larissa snorted. "You of all people should know chain messages are like mean chicks––never to be trusted!" She giggled at the comment. After her ordeal last night, that seemed to be appropriate.

Cher didn't seem to hear her. "Well, yea, but I mean, if it is true, I don't want to mess it up! You know how much I like him!"

"How wouldn't I know? You talk about him almost every time we're on the phone, or texting, or IMing, or––"

"So I'm obsessed, sue me!"

Larissa giggled. "What are you doing about it now?"

"What every smart girl would do: I'm going after him!"

"Cool," Larissa really didn't care about Cher's diabolical plan to get him by her side before the rest of the girls. Besides, why should she support the same girl who sabotaged her chances with the perfect guy?

By now, Larissa was busily scanning her huge revolving rack for a drop-dead gorgeous outfit to wow her fellow peers, even make Cher jealous, for a change.

"So do you approve of me pursuing him?"

Larissa rolled her eyes. Of course she didn't, but she told her, "Sure, go do your thing."

"Thanks! I'm totally glad you approve––not that I needed your approval anyway, but still, it's nice to feel assured. Don't you think?"

"Uh huh," Larissa was too preoccupied with a ruffled miniskirt she considered wearing to even care about what she was saying.

They were silent for some time. Larissa used this time to lay out her outfit choice of the day on her bed:

the ruffled mini, a simple pink camisole with a cropped Ralph Lauren blazer.

"So what are you doing now," Cher asked.

"Laying out my outfit," she answered nonchalantly. *But don't worry; I don't need your approval on anything!* Larissa wanted to add.

"Great! You can help me with mine too!" There was some rustling heard in the background. *It always has to be about her!* Larissa thought disgustedly. "Whatever," she muttered.

"I'm thinking miniskirt, but then I'm like, everyone else will be wearing that! Not cool. So then I want to wear––"

Larissa blocked Cher out at that point. She wrapped her cashmere robe around her torso and walked into her bathroom to run her bathwater.

"What do you think I should wear," she finally asked.

"Not sure. Anyway, I gotta go and get ready. See you later." She had her thumb already on the End button when Cher added:

"Wait, can we carpool today," she asked. "Richmond has the day off, and you know dad doesn't trust me driving by myself."

*Why can't you ask your step mom?* But Larissa knew Cher would never be caught dead with her. She hated

Linda Martin-von Seaton more than she hated her father for marrying her in the first place!

"Well, Sam is driving me today 'cause my car needs an oil change." That much was true. But then again, she never actually set a date to get it changed. "And you know Sam, he hates being late for anything!" Larissa was determined to refuse Cher's request. No way would she ride in the same car as the girl who literally made her look like a fool in front of her crush.

"Can't you talk to him for me," she begged. "My dad has an early morning meeting, and I'm not having Linda drive me in her ugly Volvo! Volvos are so nineties!"

"Well—" There was no point. Cher wasn't backing down that easily, and it was too early in the morning for an argument on such a trivial issue.

"I'll see what I can do."

But instead of Cher being grateful, she snapped, "No, I need a "yes" or "no" answer. Now!"

Larissa rolled her eyes. *What more does she want from me?* "Yes, I'll pick you up around seven thrity-ish. Sound cool?"

"Better than cool! Kisses." She hung up.

Larissa set her phone down on the marble sink counter shortly after and screamed into her loofah. *Why did I say yes?* She kept repeating in her head. But being mean to Cher would mean losing her popularity status. That's probably what's kept them so close for so long. She feared becoming a loser who would be stuck worshipping Cher and being tortured by her as well.

But maybe it was time for change. Maybe it was time for Larissa Kate Evans to finally pick and choose her own friends without Cher doing it for her. Plus, how could she respect the same person who stabbed her so deep in her heart? And she kept asking herself that question over and over again as she got ready that morning.

********

Downstairs, Larissa found her father Royce sipping freshly brewed coffee and reading the morning paper that the butler hand delivered to him at the table while Deborah, her mother, was putting together some files before heading over to her office.

"Morning, mom; morning, dad." Larissa put down her tote bag by the island and pecked her mom on the cheek.

"Morning, hon," Deborah answered. "How'd you sleep last night?"

Larissa didn't say anything when she heard her say that. When she gazed at her mother, she was busy looking down at her files. *Did she notice the bags under my eyes?* She casually put her fingers there just to make sure they weren't puffy. *I thought I put enough concealer on?*

"Lissa, darling, are you alright," her mother asked, staring at her peculiarly.

"I'm fine," she said. "I must be exhausted."

"From what?"

"Well, I hardly got any sleep last night." *Because the man of my dreams turned out to be a fake, and my so-called best friend possibly told him all sorts of lies about me, which is why he hates my guts, and Cher kissed him!* "Could be nerves."

Deborah rubbed her daughter's elongated arm. "You'll be fine; I know you will. It's just high school."

Larissa scoffed. *Easy for her to say. Back in her day, high school didn't contain backstabbing best friends!*

"Thanks," she grabbed her tote bag. "See you later." As she was walking towards the foyer, Royce called out to her.

"Aren't you taking your car?"

"About that. Is it okay if Sam drives me today?"

"But aren't you the same one saying you wanted your freedom? That's the reason we bought that car."

"I know, but I miss Sam driving me around, you know? And aren't you always telling me you get so nervous when I'm driving on my own?"

"True––" Royce peered up at Larissa from his reading glasses. "Well, you're in luck. Last I checked, he's out front, enjoying the view."

"Thanks, bye." Larissa rushed out to the motor courtyard.

"Have a great first day," she heard her mom call out. But with Cher around to be a constant reminder of last night's misfortune, she wasn't sure how "great" her first day back would be...

********

"Morning, Sam," Larissa hovered over him.

Samson put down his copy of the paper and glanced up at the girl-turned-young-lady he had served for so long. "Ms. Evans," he said. He seemed surprised to find her there. He stood and looked deep into her eyes. "I see you are still sober."

Larissa smiled and playfully hit him. "You know I'm better than that!"

"Of course, I know. I practically raised you, didn't I?"

Larissa nodded. He did help in raising her when he was first hired three years ago. Now, he didn't even feel like a driver, but more like family. "Can you drive me to school today? And maybe pick up Cher on the way?"

Samson stroked his chin. His forehead grew creases as he stared at her confusingly. "But my understanding is your parents purchased a car for you four months ago."

"Yes, but I'm still not used to driving by myself, and I'd really like to have you drive me around again. Just for today, that is."

He tipped his hat. "I'd be most delighted. I'll be right back." He rushed inside through the Service Entrance and came back out holding the keys to the Mercedes SUV in his hand. He took her tote bag from her and rushed to put them in the trunk. Larissa followed behind clutching her handbag tightly.

After admiring her reflection in her compact mirror, Larissa was finally satisfied with her appearance. *Perfect!* She thought. *I think I can pass as a Victoria's Secret model!* It helped her to think of herself as gorgeous when she compared herself to gorgeous women in society. She set her compact back in her handbag before looking up toward the driver's seat, wondering why the car hadn't moved yet.

Sam was staring back at her. "If you're done putting on your cosmetics, I would like to take you to school now."

Larissa smiled politely, even though she really wanted to slap Sam for being such a smart mouth! *After all the money my father gives to you, you still have the nerve to smart mouth me?* "We can leave now," she muttered.

"Of course," he nodded and turned in his seat. As soon as he stepped on the gas, the car glided down the private drive.

\*\*\*\*\*\*\*\*

Loraine, the von Seaton's maid who immigrated to America from Ireland answered the door. The two spoke briefly until she went inside the house. Sam waited patiently at the door, fixing his Armani tuxedo collar. Finally, Cher stepped out of the house, her wispy bob blowing with the light breeze. Sam took her metallic

Salvatore Ferragamo Gancio tote bag from her and held it proudly in his hands.

Cher smiled at him and strutted toward the car, holding her white Jimmy Choo calfskin handbag, which matched the cropped white pants she decided to wear. She also wore her Manolo Blahnik open-toed pumps with a Michael Kors camisole-classic Cher look. She looked as glamorous as a runway model as her curvaceous body continued to walk down the stone pathway from her house.

Larissa gazed at her the whole way through the tinted windows. She kept wondering how could she walk with such poise; such grace, and not look like she had an ounce of guilt for kissing her crush. Even if they weren't officially together, that still counted as 'breaking the code of girl-world'.

Sam opened the back car door on the opposite side of Larissa, and Cher slid in. He set her tote in the trunk behind them and shut the trunk door.

"Love the outfit," Larissa lied. There was really nothing special about it, but she knew Cher would ask for a compliment soon or later.

Cher had just taken out her compact. "Thanks," she answered, busily applying black MAC mascara. She finally set her monogrammed compact back in her bag and turned to Larissa. "Sorry, but the clumps in my eyelashes were very un-Tyra."

Larissa grimaced, "It really wasn't, but it's better now." *Psyche!* "Anyway, I like the outfit you finally picked.," she lied.

"I know," boasted Cher. "Isn't it gorgeous?"

Larissa loathed the way Cher always put herself on a high pedestal and put all the rest beneath her like they weren't up to her level of class. But what seemed to baffle Larissa sometimes was how Cher had changed from the fun-loving, easygoing Cher she used to be.

Everything changed the year she was graduating from middle school––the year that was supposed to be the greatest year of her life. From graduation parties until early hours in the morning to sunbathing in Central Park, sipping fresh-squeezed lemonade with her friends, even capturing her ex-crush, Wylie Paterson––though the relationship didn't last long. But when her biological mother, Janine, slept with another man, things changed after that. Cher became depressed, and that was basically the point she started treating others badly. It was a way for her to let her anger out.

In the meantime, Eric, Cher's father had made millions with his software and decided it was time to move out west for a restart in life, which was when they moved into their current residence in Mavis Gardens.

In the beginning, Cher was really starting to like her new life—maids waiting on her, butlers serving her food in bed if she felt like it, drivers to chauffer her around town, personal shoppers that kept in her style, and hanging out with celebrity children, just like her!

Life was the way it was supposed to be––glamorous and mom-free. That is, until barely two months later when Eric fell in love with Linda Martin, a divorced woman who owned a hair salon outside Malibu. Instantly, Eric fell in love with her. Before Cher could stop them from marrying, they exchanged vows. The rest is history.

"Do you feel like shopping today," Cher asked Larissa out of nowhere. She pulled out a bottle of Evian from the built-in fridge.

"Well, I don't know if I can make it,"

Cher folded her arms. "And why not?" She sipped her Evian. "Don't you know their having the private previewing of the latest fall collection at four today at Sophia's? A-lister's only!"

Larissa didn't care too much about the previewing. Whatever they were showing would be out in two months anyway.

"Don't you want to go," Cher asked.

"It's not that I don't want to go"––*Even though I don't*––"but, you see, I––" She gazed out the window, hoping for an excuse to come to her. All she saw was a cyclist cruising down Sunset and a white Camry speeding to get the green light.

"You what?"

Larissa said the first thing that came. "I just remembered my mom has a surprise planned for us this afternoon. Probably some way for us to bond better."

Cher fought back giggles. "Are you honestly turning down a chance to preview the hottest fall fashions from Europe to go somewhere with your mom?"

"Cher, you have to understand my mom and I haven't spent much time together, and she's really been looking forward to this. Please understand."

She sighed and gulped down a mouthful of water. "Well, if you can't come, I guess, I'll have to deal with, right?"

"I'm sorry. Do you forgive me?"

Cher grabbed the remote off the center console and began browsing the channels for MTV. "Sure, you're forgiven." She didn't bother looking at her.

Larissa was so befuddled. For a second, she actually thought Cher was using reverse psychology on her. But when she stared at Cher for the moment she was too pre-occupied with the episode of Made onscreen, she seemed fine. Then, Larissa giggled. *Wow! Who knew Cher would be* this *understanding? I guess deep down inside, she really does have a heart of gold!*

"What's so funny," Cher asked, looking away from the screen for a moment.

Larissa shook her head. "Nothing," she inhaled. "I just wanted to say thanks for being so understanding."

Cher raised her eyebrow at her. "Um––you're welcome? But really, there is no need to get all mushy about it." Cher grabbed the remote off the center console and changed the channel. "Besides, I prefer going to these events alone—–it leaves all the good clothes to me!"

Larissa didn't even bother retorting what Cher just said. She was too busy silently clapping for she made up such a brilliant lie, and Cher actually *believed* it! *Just think, if it worked this time, imagine all the other things I can wiggle myself out of . . .*

# 2

Sam dropped the girls off in front of Cornelius Academy, the girls' high school. Cornelius Academy is a posh coed high school located in the secluded, expensive neighborhood of Beverly Hills. The school was founded back in the 1920s by a group of Spanish missioners, who felt having a school based on Catholic education would be best for the community. But when the founders died and their children took over, they changed it to a charter school to allow all religions. Since then it has become one of the best schools in the country.

Cher and Larissa met up with their friends Tommy and Carlos at their usual fountain spot in the middle of the manicured lawn. The fountain spot was the coveted waiting area for all the students at Cornelius. It was the place to be seen! Unfortunately, thanks to Cher's power over the entire student body, only a select few (i.e., popular kids) could be seen there.

The girls set their totes down in the dewy grass before talking with their friends. "Hey, guys," Larissa saluted. "I can see the party didn't crash you guys down after all!"

Tommy chuckled. "Yeah, but, as for T.J. and Mitchell, they were wasted! But when I called Mitch this morning, he told me he'd be coming to school. He wasn't sure about T.J. His mom was ticked off when she heard he snuck out to a party!"

Cher rolled her eyes. "T.J. is so stupid," she flicked her hair out of her eyes.

"Chill, Cher," said Tommy. "It's not like he hasn't done this before. Trust me on this one, he'll be fine."

Larissa sighed. "I hope so. Anyways, we didn't have much time to talk last night"––she sat on the edge of the fountain after checking for wet spots––"so how was your summer vacation?"

"Awesome! I went clubbing in Reno, met hot chicks in Aruba , ran into *the* Barry Bonds at the supermarket––"

Carlos burst out laughing. "Stop lying man! You didn't meet no Barry Bonds at the market. Neither did you go clubbing nor did you meet hot chicks in Aruba, or whatever!" He turned to his friends and told them the truth. "All he really did was go up to his grandparents' house in Oregon for a few weeks because his *parents* were away on vacation and didn't trust him alone."

Cher giggled into her palms, being extra careful not to smudge her highly glossed lips.

"Hate to say it, Tom, but you're a really bad liar," exclaimed Cher.

"Consider sticking to your day job," added Carlos. He loved encouraging his crush of three years––even though Cher didn't know it yet.

Cher sneered. "Which is nothing!"

The two laughed even harder causing some of the students now coming in to stare and gossip to their friends. News spread fast around Cornelius, especially if it had to do with the goddess herself, Cherisse von Seaton.

Tommy started up a new topic. "So, what do you think our teachers are going to be like this year?" he asked.

"Well"––Cher tapped her chin with her manicured nail––"they're probably still boring, still dress like a cheap, secondhand rag doll, oh, and still *themselves*!" Cher received a round of high-fives for that cruel comment. Not from Larissa, of course. But Cher didn't seem to care that much––at least, she never showed she cared. She got the praise she wanted, and that was it!

"I just hope I don't get Ms. Hanson," Carlos said, scraping the grass off his Puma sneakers. "Rumor has it she goes down to the city dump every night to get furniture and junk to sell on Ebay."

Cher winced. "That is *so* gross! Is she honestly that desperate for extra cash that she needs to search the dump for stuff to sell?"

Carlos shrugged, "As long as it's not me, I don't really care what she does to get cash!" His friends laughed.

Larissa, being the kind and thoughtful person that she was, stepped in. "Don't you guys think you're being too harsh on her? Maybe that's her only hope for survival?"

"Oh yea, like you've been an angel all the time," snorted Cher.

"Excuse me?"

"You heard me! I said, you aren't the little miss pocket of sunshine like you claim to be!"

"Cher, what are you talking about?"

"Does *I go to Pepperdine* ring a bell?" But then, Cher quickly shut her mouth. What had just come over her? Could it be she was waiting for the perfect moment to finally confess the truth––or shall I say lie––she already knew?

Larissa gasped. How could she have possibly known? Unless, *Cher was the one who told Lance! She* did *lie to him just so she could get her piece of him! That witch!* "I knew it! You lied to him about me, didn't you?"

"Hey! Let's be fair now; you lied to him too."

"Yeah, but I was eventually going to tell him! You only lied so you could get him to make every jealous, as always! God I can't believe you can be this evil!" Larissa stared into Cher's eyes. They seemed focus, but deep down, they were hurt. "And to think, I called you my best friend!" She looked down at Cher's tote and stomped it into the mud. "I hope you go to hell for this!" And with that, Larissa gathered her things and left them.

And Larissa was determined to make this the last time she and Cher crossed paths––forever.

Cher stared at Larissa as she marched away from the spot they shared so many secrets for so many years.

"What was that all about," Tommy asked. "Are girls always this catty?"

But Cher didn't answer. The only answer she had was tears––and lots of it.

At first, Larissa had no idea where she'd go. Her mind was jumbled with the thoughts of Cher making out with Lance, and then figuring out she did, in fact, tell him all those lies. So for the first time in Larissa's life, she asked herself, where do I go?

*Do I go with the jocks?* Right now, they were hanging by the parking lot, throwing around a football––and nailing parked cars every now and then. There was no chance of her being accepted into that group. Besides the fact she was physically inept, the jocks only went after cheerleaders. They were out of the question.

Over by the entrance steps, she spotted The Clones, or four ninth-grade losers who idolized Cher and everything she did. They were texting each other on their Sidekicks and Blackberry's; however, they only used that as an excuse to hide what they were really doing––admiring Cher from afar, wishing they could be just like her. No way was Larissa going over there. She had had enough of *anything* dealing with Cher.

She then came across the drama club sitting underneath a large palm tree close to the gymnasium. Two were reading Shakespeare plays out of a playbook whiles the other four talked and sipped coffee out of their Starbucks venti-cups. Again, Larissa knew she wouldn't be accepted. They tend to keep to themselves.

Of course Cher had something to say about them and their attitudes (or what she called mooditudes). She assumed they were depressed and had no lives whatsoever.

"I mean, you'd think they'd go shopping if they were that depressed," she remembered Cher telling her one morning before the bell rang.

Cher popped a Life Saver into her mouth. "Wouldn't you think so?"

Larissa didn't think so. "Why can't you accept them for who they are? Not everyone is as privileged as you!" *Maybe then she'll understand why a judging person is wrong.*

But instead Cher continued sucking on her mint. "I guess you're right – oh well! I can't help it if their daddies can't afford Gucci!"

Larissa didn't want to believe Cher had just said that.

Cher hadn't noticed the shocked expression on her face and went right back to complaining about her stepmother, again.

Thinking back, Larissa felt that was probably when she really considered leaving Cher alone. She wasn't gaining anything from their friendship besides popularity, and the assurance that it would stay that way.

Now that was all a distant memory, and strangely, she was hoping that would stay that way.

Finally, Larissa turned her attention towards the dumpsters that was unofficially, and wrongfully, dubbed the "loser's corner." Basically a bunch of "normal" kids who weren't worthy enough to be Cher's friends or be popular hung out there with friends until the bell rang. She spotted a clique of girls, two blondes and one redhead, purposely throw their balled up wad of gum towards a group of girls talking. The clique were walking over to the gym when one called out to them:

"Hey! Watch where you're throwing that," she yelled, pulling up the strap of her backpack. Her friends tried to shush her, but it didn't seem to help. As Larissa observed, she noticed this girl was new.

One of the bleach blonde girls turned on the heel of her stilettos. "What are you gonna do about it?"

"What *can* she do," the other natural blonde asked.

"Well, for starters, she can shut up!" The first blonde snapped.

The redheaded examined her profile. The girl wore a Happy Bunny Shirt, dirty high-top Converses and ripped jeans. "And maybe a makeover!" Her friends laughed as they pointed out the two-sizes-too-big T-shirt, along with the faded Old Navy's with a gaping hole around her knee.

The girl stood awkwardly before them, embarrassed.

"Just leave us alone, Marissa," pleaded Tara, one of the girls the New Girl was talking to. "There's no need for this."

"Marissa, she's right. Can we just go," asked the redhead, who was fishing around her purse for something. "I don't even know why we're wasting our time with this––freak!"

The other blonde added, "Helen's right. She's not worth our time."

Marissa glared at the guy for a while until finally she said, "let's go," and shoved her into the dumpster. "And the next time you cross me, you'll wish you hadn't met me!" And just like that, she and her friends walked towards some girls in the middle of the lawn, who were sunbathing in miniskirts and bathing suit tops, even though it was prohibited. The bathing suit tops, that is.

Her friends quickly encircled her to help her get up from off the ground. "Do you need to see the nurse," asked Gia, another one of the girls standing over her.

The girl stood up, cupping her head in her hands. "I'll be okay." As she stood up, grasping onto Gia's arm for balance, she spotted Larissa staring at her. They stood there in silence for some time, unaware of the people who stood in shock after the little "show", but soon, a smile spread across Larissa's face, hoping maybe the girl would smile back.

But before she had the chance, the eight o'clock bell rang. Larissa quickly gathered up her things and raced up to the school entrance. She just had to get inside to learn more about that new girl. Perhaps she was the answer she had been searching for?

Larissa was able to make it to the admissions office on time. She was placed in the line for students with last names starting with A all the way to M. Right now, the admissions officer was on Sato Akita.

The Akita family moved from Japan when Sato was two years old. Soon Mr. Akita opened a restaurant in West Hollywood, and finally, five years since their arrival in the United States, the Akitas' eatery became a success, making them millions. He, along with Sato's five brothers and sisters, moved to their current mansion in Bel-Air.

Sato hardly spoke to anyone because he was always busy working in his father's restaurant, or studying his brain off at the Margaret Herrick Library on Sunset.

"Sato Akita," Mr. Murphy called out. Sato straightened the collar on his fitted, dark green Burberry London polo and stood. Larissa scanned his silhouette attentively. He actually looked quite attractive with the cream-colored Theory pants and white Dolce & Gabbana loafers. His hair was gelled back, accentuating his brown eyes and round cheeks. He walked into the room and closed the door behind him.

Once again, Larissa seemed lost amidst the clusters of teens gossiping around her as if they knew what happened last night. She wouldn't be surprised though––any news about Cher was worth talking about. She looked around the hall to see if she'd find her, just to see if she was just as lost and confused as she was.

To her surprise, Cher seemed as fine as ever, smiling and whispering with another one of her friends, Brittany Wellington.

Just like the majority of Cornelius Academy's student population, the Wellingtons were wealthy and well respected in society. Her father owned casinos and theme-resorts in and around Reno and Las Vegas.

They glowered at the two girls standing in front of them, hugging their paisley-print messenger bags close to their chests. Larissa recognized them as Amy Franklin and LaTanya Watkins. They were both at least two feet taller than both Brittany and Cher, which would explain why they both played Center on the girls' JV basketball team.

"How do you think she fit through the door," Brittany whispered loudly. "She's, like, taller than the Empire State Building!" The two girls giggled into their palms when Amy met their gazes.

"If you got something to say, say it to my face," she spat as she crossed her arms across her toned upper body.

Cher forced herself not to burst out laughing in her face. "I didn't say anything!"

LaTanya joined in. "Liar! We heard you talking about us!"

"Well, it looks like you'll need to visit the ear doctor 'cause we said nothing about you guys! Besides, wouldn't it make sense to ask if we were talking about someone else?"

"It would, but there's no point. You said something, and I want you to apologize, now," yelled Amy. By now, everyone's attention was on the mini-cat fight brewing at the moment.

Cher stepped closer to her, showing she was not fearful of her threats. "And if I don't?" They were eye-to-eye now, not taking their glances off each other for one second.

Larissa knew she should've gone over there to stop it. After all, it was the most logical thing to do when all of a sudden; she heard Mr. Murphy's voice from behind.

"Ms. Evans!" Mr. Murphy stood in the doorway. Everything stopped almost immediately and, suddenly, made Larissa feel uncomfortable. She quickly ducked into the crammed space, also known as Murphy's office, and hoped the whispers and ogling would melt away.

# 3

Mr. Cliff Murphy was a cute, thirty year old male with his pale brown hair usually worn long and muscles perking out from under his Robert Graham striped tee. Larissa now understood why so many girls at school had crushes on him. If only he wasn't so disorganized then perhaps those girls wouldn't freak out anytime they stepped into his office.

And that's exactly what was going through Larissa's mind at that moment.

He had loose papers and folders overflowing his small desk, empty Wawa coffee cups tossed about on the stained carpet; even the picture of him and a couple of other people––Larissa assumed they were his friends––at a local night club that was nailed to his wall was tilted to the side. What Larissa really couldn't stand was the unbearable stench of coffee grounds. She tried her best to hold her breath, but she'd always end up lasting about ten seconds before she gasped for air!

"Let me get your schedule," said Mr. Murphy and went into the room adjacent to his office and began searching for Larissa's class schedule.

Larissa sat down at the seat in front of Cliff's desk after making a thorough check for coffee-stains and other unmentionable filth. Once she was settled in, her phone buzzed in her handbag. She pulled it out, looked in the adjacent room, and when she was assured Mr. Murphy was still searching for her schedule. She flipped her RAZR open and was about to reply, when she read the name of the sender. It was Cher.

**Cher:** r u still mad about wat i said this morning?

**Larissa:** i guess i'll get over it…

**Cher:** u've got 2 believe me. i had no idea wat came over me? i just had 2 tell u the truth.

**Larissa:** shouldn't u have thought of that when u told Lance all those lies? Then kiss him just 4 ur own selfish reasons! Haven't u even thought of how hurt he'd b if he found out u only kissed him 2 make others jealous?

**Cher:** i kno wut i did wuz wrong, but plz, lissa, 4give me ur my bff

Larissa overheard Mr. Murphy mumbling something under his breath. "Is this it," he said to himself. Finally, he announced, "I found it."

**Larissa:** txt u l8ter. Murphy's cumin.

**Cher:** don't forget.

Larissa had no intention of remembering. She knew Cher would be outside their usual eating spot, Café Renee, a posh restaurant in the school's food court reserved for the popular kids only, waiting for an answer. *I've got to think up a plan to avoid Cher at all costs, but how?* Before she could think up a plan, in came Mr. Murphy, waving the slip of paper high in the air.

"It took me a while, but I finally found it," he informed Larissa, handing her the Excel document.

"Thanks," she acknowledged as she stood up from her seat.

He took a sip of his coffee from his mug. "You're welcome."

When Larissa inhaled, she took a whiff of his coffee-breath, nearly causing her to throw up all over Mr. Murphy's boat shoes. *Save me*, she pleaded.

"I hope you'll find your classes to your satisfaction." Larissa wasn't sure how to answer that. None of the classes she got each semester were to her liking anyway! So instead, she simply smiled and nodded politely.

Mr. Murphy checked his watch. Meanwhile, Larissa was able to catch a quick glimpse of the shirt he was wearing. It was flattering on him, but then Larissa's eyes passed over the splotches of what looked like blueberry jam. *What a slob! I hope this guy doesn't dress like this in front of his girlfriend . . . that is, if he can even get one looking like that!*

"Well, I won't hold you any longer," he finally said. "Your homeroom time starts in about two minutes, and once again, I'm sorry for the inconvenience."

Larissa hung her tote over her shoulder. "It's okay, really."

"I'm glad." He grinned. At least his teeth were a bit decent. "If you have any problems whatsoever, come find me, and I'll be happy to assist you."

This time, Larissa was prepared for Mr. Murphy's infamous coffee breath and held her breath for a full six seconds. "I'll be sure to do that," she said to him and promptly left the cramped space before she suffocated.

Once she was out of his office, she inhaled deeply, relishing the fresh, coffee-free air she was breathing in. *Finally! I'm free!* She then noticed the lines on both sides of the hall had dramatically shortened. Truthfully, most of them had been asked by the principal to go over to her office to receive their schedules because the counselors were taking up time. Larissa attempted to find the new girl, but sadly, she was nowhere in sight. She let out a sigh. *I guess I'll just have to wait until next time.* Then her attention went to her the schedule she had no time to look at in Mr. Murphy's office.

According to what she saw, she would be taking American Literature second period following Spanish 1, World History, Geometry, AP Chemistry, and Health. *Why would Mr. Murphy give me AP Chem? I suck at chemistry! Plus, I hate learning about it! I was never awake during the classes!* She looked at the block that told her what her first period was. *Well, at least I have homeroom first!* She crumbled her schedule into her tote and walked down the hall toward room 516, the juniors' homeroom.

*4*

Cher was sitting in the back of the room with Brittany and her other friends. The ones Cher disliked but didn't find need to torture were forced to sit in the front, far enough to be unable to hear anything she was saying. The losers, on the other hand, had to sit in a dark corner of the room. Basically, this was the part of room 516 that had poor fluorescent lighting, dusty desktops, and really tight space, so they weren't comfortable—just the way Cher wanted it.

But instead of whining about her class schedules like the rest of her friends, she sat quietly, thinking why she had to go as for as betray her best friend. *What did I see in that guy anyway? It's not like I can't get better!*

"Why would Principal Carter have me put in Physics," Cher heard Carlos ask his friends.

Tommy answered, "She doesn't make sense to begin with! Can you believe she put me in Calculus, of all subjects, when she knows I flunked Algebra II last year!"

"Well, I say it's time we get a new principal," said Brittany, looking up from her compact mirror. She was sitting behind Carlos, still fluffing her crimped blonde hair. "I mean, hello, she still wears polyester! Gross!"

"Yeah. I mean, about the 'getting a new principal' thing," T.J. blushed. He had come in late, that morning, just before they were going to homeroom. "Maybe then we'd get a better principal."

"That would be heaven," Mitchell leaned back in his chair and dreamt of the thought of having a nicer principal––one that didn't send him to detention every so often.

His friends laughed.

Cher rolled her eyes. She hated it when she wasn't included in something, and that's exactly how she felt at the very moment. *How can they be so happy and carefree while I'm stuck worrying if my best friend in the whole wide world hates my guts!*

"What do you think," Carlos asked, waving his hand in front of her face. She rapidly went through her thoughts trying to remember what was the last thing she heard her friends saying.

"Yeah, sure," she murmured.

"So you like my petition idea," Brittany asked as she put her compact back into her Yves St. Laurent handbag.

"About what?" Before she could get an answer, she noticed Larissa walking into the classroom with her eyes anywhere but at their section. *I guess that means she's still not talking to me.* She watched as Larissa scanned the room for a place to sit. Cher longed for her to look her way, but never did she once do so. *I've got to make her look over here!* "Larissa, over here," Cher called out.

Larissa did glance over, but she didn't smile or say 'hi' back. Instead, she rolled her eyes as if coming there was the worst thing in the world and trudged up to her.

"Hey, Larissa," said Cher, trying to start up a conversation. "How did the Mr. Murph thing go?"

Larissa sat down in a desk in front of Cher and began looking at her nails––not bothering to look into Cher's face. "Okay, I guess." She then began looking through her purse for a nail file. "I mean, it's not like I had fun smelling the stale coffee in his office."

"Yeah," T.J. agreed. "What is Mr. Murphy's problem anyway?" He spun his chair around and sat backwards in it. "When it was my turn to get my class schedule, he had spilled his coffee all over it!"

His friends began laughing and gripping onto their chairs to keep from falling. Some of the others who were left to watch on the sidelines began murmuring to their friends about it.

T.J. blushed. "It's not funny," he mumbled.

"Yeah, it is!" Brittany exclaimed. "Why else would we be laughing?"

She received a high-five from Cher, who temporarily forgot her dilemma with Larissa.

Larissa, on the other hand, sat there quietly and continued filing her nails.

"It gets worse," T.J. said after his friends cooled down. "Now I have to share Waldo Spinster's schedule until next week."

Waldo was one of the nerds sitting in the dark corner of the room with his other freaky friends. Cher had picked on him for some time when he first came to Cornelius two years ago, but now there was no point. He was old news.

"Ha! You have the same classes as Waldo Spit-ster?" He usually spat when he spoke because of his retainer.

"Shut up," T.J. shouted.

"But honestly, T.J., he is such a freak!" Brittany said, taking out her lip gloss. " I think there was this rumor going around that he liked me!"

Larissa pretended to be clearing her throat when in reality she was trying not to laugh at Brittany's assumption. She was right about the gossip concerning her, but it wasn't about anyone liking her. "I find that hard to believe," she mumbled under her breath.

"I totally agree," Cher added. None of them seemed to hear Larissa's comment. "I swear it looks like his mom dresses him! Just look at what's he's wearing."

They all gazed over in Waldo's direction. His two other friends, Harry and Paul were busy watching Waldo play with his Playstation Portable. He was wearing a baby blue T-shirt with "Spinster Family Reunion" engraved across the front, faded Levis that cut off right at the top of his ankles and Skechers.

"How gross is that," giggled Brittany.

Larissa didn't answer because just as she was about to ditch them to go sit by herself away from Cher and her gossip-obsessed friends, in came the new girl with the girls that had helped her earlier on. She had an ice pack pressed to the back of her head where her injury had been. After double checking Cher wasn't watching––which she wasn't ––Larissa quickly slipped away and met up the group of girls.

"Hey, remember me," Larissa asked them.

They all stared at her strangely, mainly because they knew she was one of Cher's trusted companions. For all they knew, she could be plotting to humiliate them.

"What do you want from us," Gia, basically the ringleader of the group asked.

"Well, you may not know me––"

"We know who you are, Cher's flunky!" Jade spat. "Now if you don't mind––"

All four girls brushed past Larissa and went to sit at four desks. *Cher's flunky?* Is that what people really thought of her around school? *Have I been the butt of all gossip for all this time, and I never knew it? Or maybe it was something I said?* But after truly thinking it through, it wasn't what she said; it's what she had become——and there was no one left to blame but Cher.

\*\*\*\*\*\*\*\*

"Where did Larissa go," Cher asked after finally recognizing the fact Larissa had left them.

"Let her go," Brittany snapped. "She acted all——well, loser-ish earlier!"

Cher simply rolled her eyes.

"What was up with that?" Carlos continued. "It was like she didn't even want to be here." Instead of joining in with her friends——even if it was about her best friend——she saw something beyond belief. Some of the losers——the surfer chicks to be exact——were sitting on her side of the room.

According to Cher's unnecessary set of rules she established as a way to separate the popular kids from the not-so-popular ones, no loser should cross the boundaries of a popular zone, especially if Cher was present. The surfer chicks were no exception to the rule. *What are they thinking sitting over here?* Cher glared at them in disgust. They didn't seem the least bit worried about their fate. *This is* my *territory and no one enters without permission from* moi*!* So without wasting another minute, Cher casually got up from her seat.

"Where are you going?" Brittany asked.

"Be right back," she answered coolly. "I have some *business* to handle. Don't worry, I'll tell you all the details later."

Brittany finally understood what Cher meant when she pointed her chin in the direction of Gia and her clique of friends. "Oh! Well, have fun."

Cher smiled with appreciation, which was rare––Cher wasn't the type who showed affection publicly. "Duh!" And she commenced her passage over to her next victims.

********

Gia, Tara, Jade, and the new girl, whose real name was Stella Kirkpatrick, were chatting away time, not even aware of Cher approaching them.

"So where did you say you're from again," Gia asked as she was busily fixing her shirt buttons. She was known to mix up the buttons' holes from time to time.

"Queens, New York," Stella answered proudly.

"New York," Tara exclaimed. She was sitting in front of Stella's desk. "Dude, I've always wanted to go there! Have you ever seen The Statue of Liberty? Or how about the Naked Cowboy?"

"Whoa," Stella chuckled. "One question at a time."

"I'm sorry," she pleaded. "I didn't mean to be so annoying. It just that when I was younger, my family and I had very little money, so when most kids went to

Disney World, I was home, wondering about the world around me."

"It's okay. I had to go through the same thing when my dad was laid off from work at the factory." Everything changed when her father landed a great position at his current job at a local contracting firm near San Diego.

Jade twirled a braid around her finger. "If you wouldn't mind, do you think you could take me with you the next time you visit?" Jade asked. "It's always been a dream of mine to see New York."

"Me too?" Gia asked after fixing the last of her buttonholes.

"Don't forget me," chimed in Tara.

Stella grinned with satisfaction. Perhaps this school would be different than James Madison High––maybe here she'd actually have friends! "You all can come back with me next time I visit New York. Deal?"

"Sweet! I'm so stoked!" Jade exclaimed.

Stella was confused. In fact, she had been hearing this strange language ever since she met Gia and her friends earlier that morning. "Um . . . stoked?"

"Surfer lingo," explained Tara. "It's how all the teenagers talk back in Hawaii."

"Cool," Stella marveled. "So you really like it back in Hawaii, don't you?"

"Are you kidding?  It's totally awesome over there!" she bragged.

She was good at that kind of stuff.  "The surf is the best part!"

"I-I don't really surf," Stella stammered because she was afraid maybe they wouldn't accept her into their group if she couldn't surf like they did.

"You aren't alone," Jade promised.  "I was born and raised in Oregon, so you can guess what my daily activities were."

This was comforting to Stella.  *I still have a chance to secure a spot with them.*

"I can teach if you want?" Gia proposed. "The beaches around here aren't really as great as Hawaii, but it should be good——"

"Oh! It's so nice to see a bunch of losers laughing before I make them go cryin to their mommies," they heard a voice shout out.

As soon as they found the source of the voice, the girls sneered and turned in the opposite direction.  Ever since the girls started attending school at Cornelius Academy——even if they were at various times——Cher had succeeded in making their lives miserable based only on the fact they would much rather surf and hang at the beach than go on shopping sprees and spread lies about people.

"Hello, Cher," Gia muttered.

Cher glowered into her brown eyes. "Gia, it's so nice to see you've finally removed that hideous horn off your forehead!" She snickered at her own joke.

Gia hid her face that was starting to redden. She'd had a huge zit on her forehead that Cher enjoyed calling a unicorn horn. She had been so self-conscious about it that she had even begged her mom to spend almost seven hundred dollars just to get the best dermatologist in California to remove it for her. It worked, but Cher still insisted on mocking her.

"You know, the whole 'unicorn' nonsense is really getting old!" said Jade. "Can't you come up with something else?"

"And who asked for your opinion," Cher spat.

Jade fidgeted around in her seat. Suddenly, she wasn't feeling at ease with herself.

Cher let out a snort. "Anyway, I'll just cut to chase––what are you doing on my side of the room?"

"Since when is this *your* side of the room?" Gia asked. "I don't see your name written anywhere!"

Cher shot her a cold stare––similar to the one she gave Jade earlier for talking back to her. "If you know what's best for you, you'll keep your mouth shut! And FYI, I don't need to write my name anywhere; people know who *I* am! Wish I could say the same about you!"

When Cher wasn't looking, Gia stuck her tongue out at her.

By now, Stella was really getting ticked off. She had dealt with Cher's kind back at her old school, but even they had somewhat of a good heart. It was now occurring to her that maybe Cornelius wasn't the greatest school on earth like she had hoped. It was a dictatorship––and Cher was their slave driver.

And it was time things changed.

Stella jumped up from her seat and confronted Cher with all the confidence she could collect in her body. *It's time she learns a lesson, the New York way!* "We're not obligated to move if we don't want to!" she yelled out.

At first, it came as a shock to Cher that the quiet redhead just sitting all by her lonesome actually spoke, but once it sunk in, she showed the new girl her true colors. "Were you talking to me," Cher asked as she folded her arms across her chest.

"What do you think," Stella fired back, narrowing her eyes.

Cher inched closer, expecting to frighten Stella, but she stood her ground. She'd do anything to keep her newfound friendships.

"Do you know who you're messing with?"

"No one special, that's for sure!"

Everyone was in disbelief to hear the new girl had enough guts to insult the Head Swan––a name given to her to symbolize she was the prettiest girl and dominator over the entire school——in such a way. In fact, it was even unheard of.

Although she didn't show it, Cher was beyond angry. And it was about time someone put this new girl in her place. "Okay, new girl. It looks to me you need the rundown on how things work around here."

"I don't need any help from you," Stella snapped.

Cher was getting even more agitated. Nothing was going the way she had planned it. Instead of humiliating all four of the girls for crossing into her terrain, this one person was making her look like a fool. "Listen——" Cher started.

Stella crossed her arms as well. "Stella. Stella Kirkpatrick."

"Yeah, Stella who-cares-what-your-name-is! Things may be different from wherever you're from, but this is how it goes down in *my* school!" Cher began pacing up and down in front of her. "Since you're new, I'll let you off with a warning, but the next time you dare cross my path, it'll be your last, understood?

Stella dug her nails into her palm so hard it turned her fingers pale white. The rage bubbling inside her drove her to do what she did next: she literally shoved Cher into one of the desks close by, nearly causing her to fall flat on her head.

"Don't let her push you around, Cher!" Brittany shouted. "Get up and show this chick a lesson!"

As much as she loved the support, Cher ignored her. She was way too angry with Stella to encourage it.

"Now you listen, Cher," Stella asserted, practically jamming her finger in her face. "I don't care if you run this school, or call the shots. I'm an individual, and I dance to my beat, you feel me?"

Most of the losers forced into the corner smiled in agreement. A few even started to think maybe Stella was their answer to all those agonizing days being stuffed into lockers and being pantsed coming out of the gym.

"Oh, and by the way," Stella added, "your empty threats don't scare me one bit!"

"For one thing, my threats aren't empty, but are fulfilled – every single time!"

"And when they do, I'll be waiting."

Cher shook her head, half-laughing, half-ticked. "So you think you're my biggest threat, right?"

"There's no doubt in my mind."

Cher tried her very best not to just punch Stella in the face right there in front of all those people. Besides, there was plenty of time later to really teach her a lesson. "I'm watching you, Stella." She then strutted back toward her friends at the back desks.

"Right back at ya," Stella smirked.

Cher froze, but didn't bother confronting it. She had better things to do––like coming up with a plan to get even with Stella, the new girl from hell––that is, according to Cher.

Once Cher was out of earshot and everything had gone back to order, the surfer chicks almost immediately started discussing their latest encounter with Cher. "Whoa! First day and you've already been in a confrontation with Cher," Jade said. "No offense, but that's bad news for you, girl!"

Stella scrunched her nose at Cher's turned back. She seemed to be chatting it up with her friends, as if nothing happened. "None taken, but don't worry. She's not a threat to me!" She looked her friends in the eyes. "I just can't even believe you guys would let her push you around for this long! It would have never been done in NYC!"

Gia sighed, "That's how things work around here, Stella. At least, that's how it's been since we've been here."

"Well, I think it's about time that changes; no human being should suffer like this!"

"Stella, be careful though," Tara advised. "That chick is dangerous! Purely wicked; not to be toyed with!"

"Believe me, I've dealt with worse!"

"Would you just listen for a moment," asked Gia. "If you don't want any troubles here in California, take it from someone who's experienced her wrath. Two words: not good!"

When Gia was just starting school at Cornelius, she opened her locker only to be greeted by an avalanche of guacamole, which splattered all over her body. Soon after, a bunch of kids Cher had bribed circled around her, hurling goose feathers––they were stolen from the art room––at her. As she ran out of the school, bawling her eyes out, students were chanting "chicken butt."

It took her four hours just to get the smell out of her hair! Another two to wash the guacamole stains out of her clothes. *I hope guacamole isn't in Stella's future,* she thought.

"We're only trying to save you from being humiliated!" Jade placed her hand on Stella's bare shoulder. "You're our friend, and we don't want anything happening to you."

Friend. It had been so long since Stella last heard that word. At long last, she was right: coming to California was for the better, well, minus the Cher-drama that is! "Thanks for the concern, but I'm not worried about her. I can fight this battle on my own."

"She's doomed!" Tara announced.

*Way to be supportive!* Stella thought sarcastically.

"If you say so, " Gia heavily sighed.

"Just know we'll be here for you every step of the way," Jade reassured her.

Stella grinned. "Thanks, guys."

"No problem," said Gia.

"Anyway, can we talk about something else?" Tara asked. "If I talk about Cher any longer I might puke!" She shouted this loud enough for Cher to hear.

Cher didn't seem to hear a word she said. All her friends were doing their best to comfort Cher, except Larissa who decided to keep her distance from the entire thing.

Apart from the fact she didn't want anything to do with Cher or her preppy friends, she still had to do her best to become friends with Gia and her group. And since they despised Cher and everything about her, it was the best choice to make. *But will it all work out in the long run?* And that's what appeared to the most difficult question for her to reply.

*******

"Cher, don't worry about it," Brittany stated, fishing around her purse for a stick of gum. "She doesn't know who she's up against anyway. You can totally take her with no problem!"

She waved a piece of Hubble Bubble gum in her face. "Want some?"

Cher shook her head. She avoided most things containing sugary content. "No thanks," she mumbled. What she could really go for was beating the crap out of that thing that tried to outdo her! *Who does she think she is? Coming down to my school and embarrassing me in front of my friends! Not to mention, warn me! Well, Stella, you've met your match! And trust me on this one; you'll surely regret it!*

"You seem to be happy about how things went down," Mitchell said. "But I must say, I'm really surprised."

Cher tilted her head towards her trusted male comrade. "I'm not worried at all," she told him calmly. "You see, the way I handle things is based on one rule only: show the person who's boss sooner *rather* than later!"

"Totally agreeing with you." Brittany slapped hands with Cher.

"Whatever it is, just don't get me involved," T.J. told her. "I can't stand girl-drama. It's so––pointless!"

Carlos leaned in closer to Cher's ear. "Just be careful. I don't wanna see you get hurt."

Cher quickly pulled away from him and let out a scoff. "Are you crazy? Of course, I'll be fine. This chick has no idea who she's up against."

The first-period bell rang, and Cher, Brittany, Carlos, Mitchell, Tommy, and T. J. made their way out of the classroom, talking nonstop about how funny it was to see Cher humiliate Stella. But way in the back of the pack, Larissa slowly made her way out of the room. They hadn't even realized Larissa wasn't tagging along with them like she normally did.

Larissa silently thanked God for her temporary invisibility.

# 5

Larissa walked into the doors leading into her first period: American Literature. She rushed to the back of the class as quickly as possible before the vacant desk was occupied. She noticed Cher and Brittany sitting up front towards the windows, chit- chatting about which shampoos work best with their hair. Fortunately, they never once looked up at her.

Another rule of popularity: Cher always had to be seen. Sitting in the front of the classroom was one of the many ways for her to always be noticed. Only during homeroom or free period would she pick a quiet secluded corner in which to talk with her friends and isolate any outsider that tried to interact with them. Larissa watched in half relief, half-upset as her once best friend had finally moved on. *Now all I need to do is get Gia and her friends to like me!* She then thought back to homeroom, and how they had completely blew her off. *But there's no chance of that happening. They hate me, and its all Cher's doing! If it weren't for her constantly pushing me into hurting others, maybe forming new friendships would be easier.*

Just then, their chubby teacher, Mr. Lance came into the room, holding his lesson plan and his briefcase tightly in his clutch. "Morning, class," he said in a nerdy, high-pitched voice.

Cher and Brittany let out quiet giggles into their palms. "Is it just me or does it sound like Mr. Lance have some allergy issues?" Brittany asked.

"No, he doesn't have allergy issues," Cher sneered. "He has *dork* issues!"

Brittany let out a hearty laugh, gripping the sides of her toned midsection. "Good one," she congratulated. She gave her friend a high five.

Meanwhile, Mr. Lance was busy trying to settle down his class. "Ssh," he hissed, "we have to start today's lesson, so please open the Literature textbooks on each of your individual desks."

The class pulled the books closer to them and awaited their next instructions. "Now please turn to page five fifty-seven, and we'll start discussing I Know Why The Caged Bird Sings by Maya Angelou. First of all, this book would ha––"

A knock on the door silenced Mr. Lance. He peeked through the tiny window on the door and gestured the person in.

Larissa couldn't believe her eyes when she saw the person was Stella.

"Can I help you," Mr. Lance asked as he set his teacher's book down on his desk.

Stella nodded. "Yes," she replied shyly. With all the eyes staring at her, it seemed to have made the awkward situation even worse. "Is this American Literature?"

"Why yes!" His grayish-blue eyes gleamed with happiness. "Do you need anything?"

"Actually, this is my new class."

Mr. Lance shook Stella's hand harshly. "Hello, and welcome to American Literature. My name is Mr. Lance, and I'll be your new teacher."

"Nice to meet you," she grinned. "My name is Stella Kirkpatrick."

"Very nice to meet you, Ms. Kirkpatrick." He dropped his hand from her clutch. "Where did you say you're from again?"

"Queens, New York."

"What a lovely place New York is! I remember my first time going there. It was the summer of 1973 . . ."

\*\*\*\*\*\*\*\*

Cher and Brittany couldn't stop laughing even for a minute. *What a more convenient way to disgrace Stella in front of some of the student body.* Literature was really starting to become a lot more––enjoyable.

"So she's in our class now," Brittany scoffed.

"Yep! And I bet this is going to be a fun year after all," Cher whispered back.

Brittany curled her thin eyebrow upwards. "I don't understand. I mean, we have class with *her*!"

"Oh, trust me, you'll understand––sooner than you think…"

Brittany shrugged her freckled shoulders. "Whatever. You're good at this kind of stuff, so I won't judge."

"Good." Cher looked up to the front of the classroom. Stella was still standing by the door. She seemed quite interested in Mr. Lance's long lecture about his first trip to the Met. "Can you tell me why she's wasting her time listening to Mr. Lance?"

"Who knows? She's probably using this as a way to get good grades in this class."

"You don't think she's—"

Mr. Lance's voice interrupted her. "Class," he called out.

Some of the ones still awake or not preoccupied with other activities peered up from their Literature books. "Wouldn't you love to hear about Ms. Kirkpatrick's old life back in New York?"

Then they all looked away without a response.

Cher examined her profile with her keen eye. *She's from New York? There's no possible way she was bred in the Upper East Side! Just look at her clothes!* Apart from the

Happy Bunny T-shirt, Stella wore ripped jeans and high-top Converses. She had a sweatshirt fastened around her slender waist. *Definitely a designer mistake!*

"Anybody?" Mr. Lance asked once more, a little more desperately this time.

The class still wasn't budging.

Brittany leaned in to whisper something into Cher's ear. "Is she seriously wearing Happy Bunny?" she asked. "I haven't worn those things in forever––so junior high!"

"She has to dress tacky if she hangs with the surfer chicks," Cher retorted. "And, why would you wear them in the first place?"

"I was young," said Brittany, terrified Cher might 'disown' her, or worse, humiliate her in front of all these students. "But now I know better," she hastily added.

"Thank God, otherwise I'd have to pretend not to know you!"

Brittany winced at the idea of being considered a social outcast among her peers. She shook the thought out of her mind and decided to focus on impressing Cher to ensure nothing like that would happen to her. "But honestly, shirts with captions are so *not* hot this season," Brittany analyzed like a fashion editor for *Vogue* magazine. "Doesn't she know she's a walking fashion disaster?"

Cher shrugged her shoulders. "Who cares? She deserves to be publicly humiliated after standing up to me like that"––then a conniving plan crossed Cher's mind––"and I know just how to do that!"

Brittany looked at her puzzlingly. "What are you thinking now?"

"Nothing you won't find out!" And with that, Cher raised her hand up high.

"Seriously, Cher. What do you have up your sleeve?" Brittany hated to be left out on anything.

Cher smiled her signature devilish grin. It was a grin she had taught herself to wear every time she was angry or thinking of something horrible. "You'll see," she answered in a singsong fashion.

Mr. Lance peered over Stella's shoulder and finally called on her. "Yes, Ms. von Seaton."

Cher rose from her chair before speaking. "I would like to welcome our new student to Cornelius Academy by allowing her to sit next to me during class."

The class applauded, but Cher instantly put an end to it. "Thank you, but there really is no need for that." She fixed her gaze onto Stella as if she was saying; "we meet again", and Stella did the same to her, and telepathically saying, "So we do". They didn't look away from each other even for a second!

"Well, I must say, Ms. von Seaton, offering her a seat next to you is very kind and noble of you."

Cher smiled innocently. "What can I say? I was born to serve the people."

*Now I know Cher's a terrible liar*, Stella thought.

Mr. Lance chuckled, "I'm glad." He turned back to Stella. "So what do you say, Ms. Kirkpatrick? Would you mind sitting next to Ms. von Seaton for the time being?"

Stella was silent for a moment. *How 'bout for never!* She could feel her classmates' eyes on her just waiting for what she'd say next. She recognized most of them from homeroom earlier on, which obviously means they all witnessed Cher and her nearly engaging themselves in a major fistfight.

There was no point in refusing the offer now. That would only make her look like a chicken, and that's the last thing she wanted these rich snobs to think of her.

It was then she took notice of Cher. She mouthed to Stella *you don't scare me!*

Stella narrowed her eyes. *Okay, Cher. You asked for it—it's war!* She turned back to Mr. Lance with her shoulders rolled back and her small A-cup chest puffed out. She almost resembled a cadet about to take orders from its leader. "I'd love to," she announced.

Soon after, the entire class froze. No one moved; no one made a single sound, and it started to put Stella in an awkward position. *Did I make the right choice*, Stella thought.

"Excellent," Mr. Lance broke through the silence. "I think you've made a fine choice for a sitting partner."

"So you think," Stella mumbled.

Stella set her worn messenger bag next to her desk and folded her hands.

"Well, class," said Mr. Lance, "now that we––" The telephone rings interrupted him. He picked up the call. "Hello…urgent call…of course, I'll be there soon." He hung up and turned to his class. "I'll be right back, class. Please feel free to talk with each other while I'm gone, but try and keep it down." He raced out of the room.

Once Larissa was sure Mr. Lance had left, she quickly glanced over at Stella. To her surprise, it looked as if Cher and Brittany were actually having a normal conversation without laughing or pointing at her! *Is it me, or has Cher finally decided a life of mocking others isn't the road to happiness?* Sadly, Cher is far from that, my friend––far, far away from that.

Stella sat silently in her seat watching the clock every second it ticked. Cher and Brittany appeared to be too worried about their conversation about whether slides were the new 'it' thing, or flats were still cool. But a small laugh coming from behind Stella's seat––Brittany had to move to accommodate Stella––broke the quiet in that corner. It began to make her feel self-conscious, and a little awkward, too. *What on earth could they be giggling about?* She stared down at her ensemble. *I think I picked a pretty decent outfit to wear. Or maybe it's my shoes?* She took a peek at them. There was nothing out of the ordinary about them, except for the couple of grass stains she acquired this morning, but other than that, nothing. *If it isn't my shoes, what are they laughing at?*

Soon, she felt a razor-sharp fingernail dig into her back. She turned to meet the gaze of the person who did it. It was Brittany.

"Yes," Stella said irritably. "Oh, and by the way, I don't appreciate you stabbing me with your manicure!"

Brittany shrugged. "And I should care, why?"

Cher coughed loudly to keep from laughing so hard. She never once looked in Stella's direction.

"Anyway," Brittany said, "where did you get that backpack? Cher and I were just talking about how–– vintage it is. Very sixties!"

"And word on the street is sixties is coming back," Cher lied. The two girls cackled after that joke even though it wasn't that funny.

Stella remained silent and lowered her head, allowing her curly red hair drape over her face. She hoped this might act as a place of hiding from these girls. Too bad she couldn't hide there forever.

Cher slapped Stella's arm to get her attention again. "You never answered her question, loser," she spat. "Where––or better yet *why*––would you buy that pack?"

Stella mumbled something under her breath.

"I can't hear you," Brittany singsong, cupping her hand around her ear.

"A thrift store, there, are you happy," she shouted over most of the voices in the classroom.

Some stopped to see what was going on, but Cher shot them all icy glares advising to mind their own business or else.

"Thrift shop?" Brittany cried out. "You mean you actually shop in those things!" She laughed even harder and grabbed onto Cher's arms to keep from tumbling over. On most occasions, Cher would've told her to back off, but she was having such a good time tormenting the new girl, she didn't seem to care.

Stella was starting to feel offended. *I mean, what's wrong with thrift stores? They have some really cool vintage stuff there. I mean, aren't these girls into fashion and junk?*

Then an impeccable idea entered her thoughts.

She cleared her throat and bravely said to Cher, "Well, seeing as I'm not a rich, snot-nosed prep like you girls, I have no choice but to shop at a thrift store!" she snapped. "It's a New York thing. You girls wouldn't understand." *Not that they understand anything,* Stella wanted to add, but chose to just keep it in her mind.

The girls stopped their giggles and instantly gave her the dirtiest look she had ever gotten. In contrast, Stella smiled innocently as if nothing was wrong with what she had said. And nothing was wrong with it, considering all the bad things Cher had done to her in the matter of one morning. And it was about time someone showed Cher she wasn't the boss.

Note: I'm keeping score of this juicy catfight throughout the entire ordeal, so be on the lookout for your favorite side! Here are some points to start off:

### Cher and Brittany's awful insults: 0 points.

### Stella and her clever humor: 2 points.

Cher got annoyed. No one—and I mean no one—had ever had the guts to talk back to her like Stella had. But what really ticked Cher off was the fact Stella never seemed to be out of insults. She was like a never-ending cannon always firing swears at Cher. *Does she have a clue as to whom she's dealing with? Has it ever occurred to her she's messing with the meanest and richest chick on the West Coast? The same chick who isn't afraid to beat her up right here; right now! Maybe then some sense would be knocked into her thick skull!* She looked up from her nails. Stella was turned back in her seat and had her gaze fixed on the chalkboard. *Well, if she can't figure it out for herself, I guess I'll have to do it for her!*

"I guess you're right," Cher replied suddenly.

"Huh?" Stella and Brittany asked in unison.

"Of course! You aren't like us . . ." She brought her head closer to Stella's. "You're just a low, poor, filthy invalid, who thinks she's all that just because she was born and bred in New York!"

Stella shifted in her chair.

Cher knew now was the time to go in for the kill. "You don't have what it takes to be like me so don't even bother getting back at me!"

**Cher's hurtful words: 6 points.**

**Stella being burnt to a crisp: back to 0.**

Stella was nearly in tears and had to suck them back in with a calm deep breath before Cher started mocking her again. She was starting to believe that maybe her friends *and* Cher was right. *I can't fight this on my own. She's just pure evil. There's no way.*

Brittany had her eyes fixed on Stella too. "So why don't you leave being fabulous to those who really are!"

Stella just couldn't get it. What was it about her that Cher didn't like? "Why do you hate me so much? I don't even know you!"

Cher chuckled. "How cute, but, the thing is, it's not like I'm being mean to you. It's just that you chose to ridicule me in public."

"But you don't even know me?"

"And so? I have all I need to know right in front of me!"

"What are you talking about?"

"Well," Cher eyeballed her jeans, "for one thing, the ripped jeans tell me you don't have enough money to pay for tailored pants."

"And your hair needs a rinse and conditioner, ASAP!"

"But then again, she probably can't even afford the shampoo bottle!" Cher and Brittany exchanged high fives and laughed.

"LOL, Cher!" Brittany gasped. "You hit it right on the money!"

Cher abruptly stopped. "Oops, maybe we shouldn't say that!" She bit her lower lip to stop from giggling.

"Why?" Brittany seemed really baffled.

"Because our friend, Stella, here doesn't know what money is!" Cher gripped her stomach and tilted her head backwards while Brittany clutched the back of her chair to keep from falling.

Stella wiped the tears away from her emerald green eyes. Never had she been so insulted in her life. Sure, there were the catty, vicious girls back at James Madison High, but they kept it at laughing when she walked down the hall. Even then, they were just as poor, or less fortunate, like she was. "Why do you guys make being poor sound so terrible," she asked finally.

"Well, it's certainly not a good thing!" Brittany spat. "You've already proven that pretty well, if you ask me!"

"Maybe that's your opinion—" Stella was interrupted.

"It's not an opinion," interrupted Cher, "it's a fact!"

Stella had just about enough of this. "If it is, prove it!"

"Too late!" Brittany inputted, smearing on a swipe of bubblegum-flavored lip gloss.

"What's that supposed to mean?"

"I'll show you," and Cher stood up, dragging Stella along to the front of the classroom. "Class," she announced. The whole class looked at her. "I have someone here today that you all may know by now." She pointed at Stella. "Her name is Stella."

As a joke, one guy shouted, "Hey, hot stuff!"

"Need someone to float your boat," another yelled out.

"I can really rock your world," the third boy hollered. His other friends whistled and howled like a pack of perverted wolves.

Cher rolled her eyes and said, "Guys, please. How many times must I tell you, no girl on the face of this Earth will be interested in you if you continue to use those lame pickup lines?"

"Says who?"

"Says me!" Stella shouted out. "You're not even that cute!" Raul, one of the guys goofing around, shot up with intentions of punching Stella, but Cher calmly raised her hand to stop him.

"Raul, sit down!"

"I don't gotta listen to you!"

"You do now!" Cher left Stella to stand-alone up front as she shoved Raul into his seat. "And stay there," she snapped before flipping her hair and walking back up to the front. "Now that we've taken care of that problem, can anyone tell me what is wrong with Stella?"

One person raised her hand. It was Haley Johansson.

Haley was rich and famous, just like the majority of the student population. Her parents were record producers for Hightower Records in Hollywood, one of the hottest record labels in all the country. They signed artists like Cher's absolute favorite, Jo-E and other well-known singers.

Cher pointed at her, and she got up to talk.

"Well for starters, look at her shirt!" Haley pointed it out with her manicured finger like it was poison. "It just screams K-mart!"

Stella began to blush while the class laughed at her mockery.

"The 'K' meaning "Know Fashion," shouted Chloe from her seat in the back.

"But the 'know' you're talking about is spelled n-o," her best friend Mimi corrected.

"Duh! It's called a pun! My dad says those things all the time!"

Mimi pondered on it for some time. "Oh! That was *totally* clever! No wonder you're in advance Literature!"

"Hello! You're in advance Literature too," Chloe rolled her eyes. Sometimes, her best friend could be so clueless about the world around her. One time she asked if candle wax was equivalent to the earwax humans get! Stupid, I know.

"Oh yea," she cocked her head to the side. "That makes us *both* smart!"

Chloe purposely banged her head into her palm and began swearing under her breath.

Okay....

Larissa watched in horror as another student raised his hand to say what they thought was wrong with Stella.

It was Clyde Collins.

Clyde is what you would consider a preppy, Lacoste-polo-wearing, blonde-haired, sweet-talking, Miata-convertible-driving cutie! Although he wasn't much of a lady's man, he was still adored by a select few. He also stood up to talk.

"Don't get me wrong; Stella's a pretty girl—"

Brittany interrupted as she made her way up to the front of the room with Cher. "Yeah, so is a baboon's butt!" The class laughed at her joke. Stella blushed even harder.

Larissa was starting to feel even guiltier. *Why am I letting this girl be tormented like this? No human being should go through this kind of treatment!* She could see tears welling up in Stella's eyes, the sign of pain and defeat. *I have to stop it.* Then she stopped herself. How on earth would she able to stop this torture without losing her spot on top of the high school social ladder? Would she be even worthy enough to be seen in Cher's presence?

Clyde sat back down. He really didn't have much else to say.

"Anyone else," Brittany peered out to the crowd. Everyone sat in their seats, waiting to see what would happen next. "In that case, I have something of my own to share."

Cher raised her eyebrow. "Like what?"

Brittany quickly raced over to the desk at which Stella had been sitting and snatched up her pack. "Last and certainly not the least, we present to you," she held out her palms, Vanna White-style.

By now, Cher had an idea of where this was going. She took the bag away from her and finished, "The awful, torn, and, not to mention, hideous sixties messenger bag!" She used her fingers to expose the gaping hole at the bottom.

Larissa watched Stella's facial expressions as she heard the whole class laughing at her expense. It pained her even more that she couldn't build up the nerve to get up and save her. But before she could do anything, a small container fell out of the hole and crash-landed on the tiled floor. She glanced down at the floor and almost immediately knew what it was.

Sadly, Cher knew what it was too. Stella tried to snatch it up before anyone could see, but it was too late.

Cher had beaten her to it.

"What's this?" Cher asked as she examined the bottle. She displayed it to the class. They stared at it blankly.

Brittany noticed the bottle too. "Hey, Cher. I know what this is," she exclaimed as if it were a new discovery.

"Me too!" Cher shouted out loud. "Looks to me like someone is getting high off prescribed medication!" At first, half the classes' mouths dropped in shock. But after a while, they laughed, and some even clapped, at Cher's discovery.

Larissa was shocked beyond belief. First, she wasn't sure if what Cher was saying was even *remotely* true. Secondly, Stella didn't show any evidence she took drugs. And finally, she was really disappointed in Cher's actions. Never had Cher worked so hard to put down a new kid. Could it be Cher was feeling daunted by Stella's boldness?

Brittany ran back to her desk to pull her Sony digital camera––she always carried it around in case something MySpace-worthy came up––out of its leather Coach pouch. She ran in front of the pair, holding it up. "I am so posting this picture on my website tonight," she shouted. "Say *busted!*"

Cher wrapped her slender arm around Stella's shoulder and struck a Teen-magazine pose while Stella stood there idly, mortified by what was happening to her. *Kill me now!* Stella pleaded.

"Busted," Cher shouted. Brittany snapped the photo and waited until it was displayed on the tiny screen.

Cher examined it before walking back over to Stella to show her. "Isn't this a lovely picture," she asked her. Stella couldn't speak. She was too busy crying her eyes out.

"This would look fabulous posted on the web underneath my new MySpace headline: <u>New girl has Old Interests: Prescribed Meds Found in Backpack. Check My Pics for the Details</u>!" The girls began laughing loudly, just imagining how many hits Brittany would get on her MySpace, and how disgraced Stella would feel.

The two clone members came strutting up to them, carrying their matching Fendi purses.

"You should really stop," Mimi suggested to Stella. "It'll really degrade you in the long run."

"If your parents don't have enough money, I can talk to my daddy, and maybe he can pay for your admission into the best rehab this country has to offer." Chloe offered. She seemed genuinely concerned.

That's the most concern she got all morning.

"I don't do drugs!" Stella screeched.

Cher walked over to the girls. "Oh, but we found the evidence that what you're saying is a blatant lie!" She flashed the container for proof.

"That doesn't mean anything!"

"OMG, she's in denial," Mimi gasped. "Isn't that, like, bad?"

"Are you sure you don't want me to talk to my dad? He can help you." Chloe said yet again.

"For the last time, I don't take drugs!"

"How sad," said Cher, "the symptoms are already kicking in. She can't even remember if she takes drugs or not?"

Brittany set down her spiral notebook she had just gotten on a nearby desk. "Now, if any of you would like copies of these embarrassing photos, please line up and write your name down in this notebook." Nearly the entire class stood up and got in line to sign their names.

Meanwhile, Brittany joined Cher just in case she needed back-up.

"So Stella," Brittany began, "now that we know your secret and publicly mocked you, have you finally realized my girl, Cher isn't the coward you think she is?

Stella glared up at them. *Cher hasn't won this yet. She has no idea who she's up against.* "You want me to just give in to you just like that, so that you can go back to picking on me and my friends whenever you choose?"

"Duh!" Cher snorted. "Now just get it over with so we can resume class."

"Excuse me, but I'm not done!"

"Then out with it, brat," snapped Brittany.

"FYI, this is the last time you and Brittany torment my friends, you understand. And as for me, if you dare cross my path again, you'll regret the day you were born! Then you'll see that there *is* someone just as good as you out there!"

The look on Cher's face was all Stella needed to know Cher wasn't used to this kind of treatment from her victims. That's *it! This is the final straw for her,* thought Cher. And without any second thoughts, Cher slapped Stella hard across the face.

Stella paused for a moment, pressing her hand to where Cher just touched. "Oh yeah right!" Stella shouted, and with that she slapped Cher back.

The whole class was so stunned by the noise they stopped their conversations. Nobody knew what had happened. They had only heard something loud. And it wasn't the slaps.

"OMG times two!" Chloe shouted. "Stella just slapped Cher!" Everyone let out gasps. Larissa especially. *She didn't do it! No! No! No! No! No! No!* No! *Stella, why did you do that? Now Cher is going to kill you! Oh no! And I can't do anything about it!* She then looked over at the three girls. *I just hope Stella will at least make it out of here alive!*

Brittany and Cher were in a state of shock. Never had anyone laid a finger on her in that manner. No one.

Stella looked around the room. The eyes of some were bulging out of their sockets, while others had their jaws hanging down. She then turned back to Brittany and Cher, who were still glaring at her.

"I can't believe it! I cannot believe it!" Cher wailed at the top of her lungs.

Stella was trying to calm her down.

"Cher, I'm sorry," she begged. "I don't know what came over me." And honestly, she didn't. She was just so angry, her emotions took over and *boom* her hand whacked across Cher's face.

"Of course you did, otherwise you wouldn't have done it, idiot!"

"But Cher—"

"Just shut up, you piece of crap!" Cher stormed up to Stella, stared at her for a split second and then smacked her reddened cheek once more. "The next time you put your filthy hands on me, I swea—" That was when Mr. Lance walked in.

"Took him long enough," whispered a girl sitting with her friend towards the back.

"Yea, but, if he came sooner, he would've interrupted the good parts," her friends responded. "There's no way I would want to miss Cher being slapped in the face!"

The girl nodded and giggled. "You've got a point."

Mr. Lance first saw Stella rubbing the side of her face in pain. Then he saw Cher, who was glaring at Stella, and finally he saw Brittany, who was trying to act natural.

"Is there something going on that I should know about?" Mr. Lance asked. The tiny plump man turned to the class. The class sat quietly with their hands folded on their desks.

Cher spoke up. "Oh, nothing!" She exclaimed casually. "We were just . . . discussing the next story in our chapter." She turned to her classmates. "Right?" She batted her long fake eyelashes.

The class nodded their heads.

"She is such a good teacher!" Chloe commented.

"Totally," Mimi added. "I so learned more about the story from her! She made it so much fun."

Cher gritted her laser-whitened teeth together. "That's enough," she grumbled.

A grin appeared across Mr. Lance's oily face. "That's good," he commented. "It sounds like you may have a promising career in teaching someday, Ms. von Seaton."

Cher let out a fake giggle. *Yeah right! I can't imagine myself becoming a poor high school teacher like you, driving station wagons and fuel-efficient cars around town! Besides, I have dreams of modeling or acting! And even if I wanted to teach, why would I bother teaching literature?*

"Anyway," said Mr. Lance, "sorry I took so long on the phone."

"No one cares," muttered Raul to his friends. They snickered at the comment.

Mr. Lance didn't hear him and began speaking again. "Anyway, enough about my problems——"

"Seeing there are too many to count," hushed Cher.

Brittany snorted.

"Let's get back to our work," Mr. Lance announced.

Larissa watched as Stella slowly walked back to her seat, pressing her hand close to her cheek. *It's now or never,* she thought. She slowly shot up from her orange-colored chair, hoping this wouldn't be the biggest mistake of her life.

"Uh . . . Mr. Lance," she called out. Soon Stella, Mr. Lance, Cher, Brittany, and the rest of the class were all staring at her. *Nice one, Evans! Now everybody is staring at you!*

Mr. Lance turned away from the chalkboard. "Yes," he answered. Larissa took a quick glance over at Cher. Cher was glaring at her, which made Larissa feel very uncomfortable and sick to her stomach. To avoid any vomit bubbling its way up her esophagus, Larissa turned away from Cher and began to speak again.

"Is it okay if Stella sits next to me instead?"

"If it's okay with Cher and Stella. After all, it was Cher's idea!"

Cher looked over at Larissa, pouting her lips. "And I'd be so heartbroken if Stella left me and Brittany," she lied.

"Yeah, but I'm willing to move," Stella said almost too quickly.

Cher shot her an icy stare. "Shut up and let me handle this!" Cher muttered. "Or are you already giving up?" Cher's eyes twinkled at the thought.

"Well, no, but as for now, I'm done with you!" She tilted her head up front. "I'd be happy to move."

"Then it's settled!" Mr. Lance shouted out. "Stella, you may sit next to Larissa."

"Thank you." She quickly grabbed her bag off the ground and snatched her container out of Cher's clutch. Some of the students, including Cher and Brittany, snickered. Stella ignored them and headed straight to the seat next to Larissa without turning back. *I'm free at last!*

# 6

Stella stuffed her medication––which was really for occasional migraines she got–into her backpack before setting it down next to her new desk. As she was about to sit down, Raul slid the chair back with his feet, causing her to fall flat on her butt. The whole class saw the grieving Stella on the ground, struggling to get up, and then they all began to laugh hysterically.

Even though Cher found that trick to be one of the oldest ones in the book, she still laughed along with Brittany.

"Nice one, Raul," she shouted out.

Larissa assisted Stella when she was still struggling to get up. "Are you all right?" Larissa asked once she was off the ground.

"I'm fine," Stella stated softly. "Thanks . . . uh . . ."

"Larissa." She stuck out her hand.

Stella smiled and held her hand out too. "Stella."

"Gross! Larissa just touched her hand!" Mimi said.

Larissa paused. *Oh man! This is only the beginning. First mocking, then before I know it, I'm banished from Café Renee to Chicke-Dee's! Fried chicken heaven, here I come!*

Although Mr. Lance had been trying to ignore the sound before, he turned around from the chalkboard when he figured it was getting out of hand. He noticed Raul and the rest of the class chuckling nonstop.

"Mr. Raul!" he shouted. The whole class abruptly stopped laughing and faced front. The Latino guy looked up from Stella, who was blushing in her seat.

"Yeah, Professa Lance?"

Did I forget to tell you Raul is an aspiring rapper?

"That's Mr. Lance to you, homeboy!" The class began to snort some more. I mean, come on! It's weird to hear your teachers talking like you! It's like your parents trying to fit in with your friends! Creepy! "Say you're sorry to this young lady this instant!"

He rolled his eyes but apologized. "Sorry," he teased. His other classmates snickered. Once he was satisfied, Mr. Lance went back to writing on the chalkboard.

"Raul, why don't you kiss her hand too?" Andre, another one of his rapper friends joked.

Raul laughed. "Good one!" Raul leaned over to snatch up Stella's hand, and he literally licked it.

"Ew," Stella screeched.

Mr. Lance turned back around. "Mr. Sanchez, if you can't behave yourself, I'll send you to the office!"

"Sorry, I'll behave."

"Good." Then he was back to lecturing.

Yawn!

Stella was getting so upset, she could barely think straight. First, Cher and Brittany had found a way to embarrass her in front of the whole class, and she couldn't do anything about it. Now, Cher had made everyone believe she was on drugs. And on top of that, Raul and his stupid friends were harassing her!

She looked down at her favorite pair of jeans. They were covered with dust from the ground. *Great!* Stella thought in dismay. She peered up at the front of the class. *I think I can brush it all off without Mr. Lance noticing me!* Stella got up from her seat and began brushing the dust off. She shook her behind a little; hoping most of the dust would just brush off on its own.

"Look, fellas!" Raul whispered to his friends. "We got ourselves a little show going on!"

Stella stopped short. *What the heck is he talking about,* she thought. She turned to confront him. "Excuse me?"

"A show! As in, Las Vegas show? Aren't you showing us what you got," he asked with a sly smirk on his face.

*That's disgusting!* Stella thought. *I don't even like this guy! He's so . . . perverted!*

Larissa was getting tired of Raul picking on Stella, so she spun around in her seat to give him a piece of her mind. "Leave her alone, Raul!" Larissa commanded. "You're such a perverted loser!"

Raul gazed at Larissa's curvy structure. "I just love to love women," he leaned in closer to skim the back of his hand against Stella's butt.

"Dude, stop," Stella whisper-shouted.

Raul then went into Broadway-mode. "Why can't you see I am nothing without you?" He doubled checked Mr. Lance was still writing. He was. That was Raul's cue to stand up. "Come," he grasped Stella's hand tightly, "and together we'll sell drugs to the needy!" He snickered as his friends high fived him for a job well done.

"Rich performance, man," Andre congratulated.

"Leave me alone," hissed Stella, and then she sat back down.

Larissa spun around in her seat once again. "Why don't you just give it a rest? She doesn't like you."

Raul paused for a moment. "You know you wouldn't be saying all this to me if you had danced with me at Dante's pool party last month." Raul leaned across his desk. "We could've hit it off last summer."

"Oh really?"

"Yeah, girl. I felt it. It's like we had that connection, 'na mean?"

Larissa rolled her eyes and leaned in closer to Raul's face. "Listen, Raul. The only action you'll be getting from a girl is playing seven minutes in heaven with your little sister's Barbie dolls!" And just like that, she flipped her golden mane and sat forward in her seat.

"Oh, she told you, man," Mike giggle-shouted.

Mr. Lance turned around again. "Now that's enough, Mr. Sanchez!"

"That wasn't me! That was—"

"Wait, say no more," Mr. Lance butted in, "'it wasn't my fault! It was my friends!' Isn't that how it always goes?"

"But this time it seriously wasn't me! It was—"

Mr. Lance cut his explanation short. "Spare me." Then he spun back around to the chalkboard.

Some kids, including Larissa, Stella, and Raul's friends, giggled underneath their breath. Raul rolled his eyes and sat back in his chair.

"Busted, " sighed Larissa over her shoulder.

Raul ignored and shooed her away. "Shut up and turn around!" he folded his arms, "All ya'll women are the same," he placed his feet up on his desk and leaned back. "Tell your home girl over there I don't need her. She don't got back anyway!"

Raul was simply being bitter because both Larissa and Mr. Lance told him off.

It had been about ten minutes since Raul last talked to them, and already Larissa wasn't paying attention. As always, the lecture was boring her out of her mind. What was really occupying her thoughts at the moment was Stella. After all, she had accomplished in one day: confronting Cher during homeroom, slapping Cher across the face in Literature, and showing up at school in the first place, it was really starting to look grim for her as far as making new friends went. *Will her peers ever accept her? I have to find a way to help! That way I can prove to Cher I don't need her in my life in order for me to become popular! Maybe she's the answer I've been searching for so long.*

Larissa quietly ripped a piece of paper out of her notebook, grabbed her fuzzy, pink pen out of her tote and was about to write Stella a note when she saw her cell phone light up in her open purse. Swiftly, she pulled out her cell and ducked her head low. When she flipped it open, she found it was a text from Cher. It read:

**Cher:** ANSWER ME RITE NOW LARISSA! WE NEED 2 TALK PRONTO!!!!!!!

Larissa was terrified. *What if she's asking me why I offered to let Stella sit next to me?* With that in mind, she was just about ready to hit Ignore when she stole a peek over at Cher. She also had her head bowed, pretending to read the book they were discussing. Suddenly, Larissa felt something being thrown at her. She spun around and found it was Raul . . . again.

"Sending text messages during class, eh?" he asked in a soft tone. "That can really get you in trouble with Carter."

"What do you want now?" Larissa grunted.

"Hey, don't be so feisty. I'm just trying to help a friend in need!"

"Well, I don't need any help, especially from you," she shut her phone again. "And besides, this text has nothing to do with you, so mind your own business!"

Her phone lit up. It was Cher again.

**Cher:** LARISSA KATE EVANS WHERE R U? I SWEAR IF YOU DON'T TEXT BACK I'LL NEVER TALK 2 U AGAIN!!!!!!!!!!!!

Larissa rolled her eyes. She was used to Cher making stupid promises she'd never follow through on. Like that time she'd supposedly promised Larissa she'd buy her a pair of the new espadrilles everyone at school was ordering from Milan. She even promised they'd get matching pairs!

Cher claimed to have flown out to Milan one weekend back in tenth grade with her dad just to purchase those shoes because apparently the boutiques in Milan had the best quality. When she came back, she had bought those espadrilles, but there was none for Larissa. Of course, Cher came up with some excuse for not buying them.

"They were out of stock," she told Cher on the following Monday when she came back showing off her new shoes to everyone. "I was even lucky to get these when I did!"

"But you promised," pouted Larissa, on the verge of tears.

Cher was getting agitated. "Look! I told you I couldn't find two pairs of espadrilles, so deal with it!"

Larissa jumped when Cher snapped at her. *That's all I ever hear. Deal with it! Deal with it! Deal with it!* Larissa said mockingly in her mind. *Can't she think of anything better to say? Like, I don't know, sorry!!* She wiped away a single tear rolling down her flushed cheek.

Cher put her arm around her friend's neck after realizing her words were hurting her. "I'm sorry," she pleaded. "Forgive me?"

*Of course not! Not after you promised me you're buying those shoes when in reality you were only worried about yourself! Why on Earth would I want to forgive you?*

"Already forgotten," she smiled. And that's another habit she always did.

Larissa always let Cher push her around.

If Cher told her to jump, she jumped! If Cher told her to run, she'd run. And if Cher told her to deal with something, she had to. In fact, that's what every student at Cornelius Academy had to do in order to be left alone by Cher.

Later on, she found out Cher didn't go to Europe with her dad, nor did she buy the espadrilles in Milan. Instead, she had ordered them from a boutique in Barcelona and sent to the Plaza where she had stayed for Fashion Week. I guess you could say that was the first time Larissa considered breaking off their friendship, but she waited so long because she loved her power and popularity. At times, she felt bad she was using Cher like that, but then she'd remember how Cher always used her.

Then it seemed okay after that.

And she's basically been doing that ever since.

That is––up until now.

This time she heard "Psst!" from behind her. *Please don't let it be Raul! Please don't let it be Raul! Please don't let it be . . .* She slowly turned around and saw the one person she didn't want to see. "What is your problem?" Larissa whispered. "Can't you see I don't need your help?"

"Oh, come on, girl," Raul said. "At least give me a chance."

Larissa rolled her eyes. "I have a name, you know!"

"Sorry, *Larissa*," he enunciated. "Look, I can see that you're worried and don't know what to say. Let me just help you."

Larissa was silent for a moment as she glimpsed at Cher. She was in the midst of typing what looked like another text message. Sure enough, Larissa's phone lit up again, but she didn't read the message right away. Instead, she glanced at Raul, who was pleading with his big brown eyes. *Man, he'd better not mess up!*

"Okay," Larissa said, "maybe I can give you *one* chance to prove me wrong."

"Excellent!"

Larissa peeked over at Cher once more and handed the phone to Raul when she noticed Cher's head was still ducked down.

"What are you going to say?"

"Don't worry about that," Raul smooth-talked. "Just know you're homeboy got it covered!" Usually when he said that, he didn't have his plan all worked out yet!

"I can't believe I'm saying this, but . . . I trust you."

Raul smiled. "I'm glad you're finally seeing it my way!" He flipped open the phone and began searching for the latest text message from Cher.

*What have I gotten myself into?* Larissa said in her mind as she turned back in her seat, suddenly feeling the urge to puke. *Maybe if I go to the nurse right now, I'll be able to get out of this boring class . . . and this horrible situation I've just gotten myself in!*

Raul had finally found the message and was about to reply to it when Andre, leaned over. "Yo, man," he said. "What are you gonna say?"

Raul paused. *I didn't think about that!* he thought. He rubbed the back of his neck nervously. "That's a good question . . ." That's why you never put your trust into a boy who clearly has no aim in life whatsoever!

\*\*\*\*\*\*\*\*

Cher had still not gotten a reply from Larissa, and she was becoming ruthless. *How long does it take someone to reply to a simple text message?* Cher asked herself. *Unless she's ignoring me!* She paused. *No, she wouldn't dare! She's knows the consequences, and she knows I'm capable of making them happen! There's just no way she'd ignore me!*

Brittany noticed that Cher was still staring at the screen. "She hasn't replied yet?" She asked as she stared down at her friend.

"Nope."

"What's her deal?"

"I don't know." Cher shrugged her shoulders and glanced over at Larissa. She was paying attention to the lecture––hard to believe, seeing as how practically the entire class was dozing off. *She is ignoring me! How can she do this to me? After all I've done to make her popular and get her name on all the VIP lists for the hottest nightclubs in the greater Los Angeles area, this is my reward?*

"What is she doing," Brittany whispered, chewing on her pen.

"Paying attention!"

"Ew," Brittany whispered coarsely. "She actually *likes* this class?"

"I know, hard to believe!"

"Maybe she's ignoring you?"

Cher narrowed her eyes. "That's what I'm starting to suspect."

"What are we going to do about this then?"

"I'm not sure . . . all I know is she'd better not try this with me again 'cause if she does, I'll . . ." Suddenly Cher's phone vibrated. She quickly flipped open her LG enV phone and noticed there was a text message from Larissa (well, Raul).

**Larissa:** hey Cher! Sorry I couldn't reply in time. I was paying attention so much; I didn't notice my phone light up.

"It's her," Cher announced.

Brittany grew angry. She was secretly wishing Larissa wouldn't reply back so that Cher would be mad, and she'd still have an assured spot at the top. "I thought you just said she was looking at her book or something."

Cher shrugged. "Maybe she finally took the time to check her missed text messages," she looked down at her phone, "and it's about time too!"

Brittany rolled her eyes and tucked her hair behind her ear. "Probably . . ." She took the pen out of her mouth and held it like a fairy wand instead.

Cher's head popped up. "Probably what?"

"Nothing." Brittany shook her head and continued to look up at the board. "All I'm saying is a lot can change in five minutes."

Cher scoffed. "Not much!" She rolled her eyes and ignored Brittany.

Brittany shrugged it off. *I tried to help her! So now if Larissa ends up doing what I think she's planning on doing, she can't blame me for warning her!* Then she went back to spacing out. Cher replied to the message.

**Larissa:** hey srry it took so long 2 reply.

**Cher:** wutever. ur forgiven.  oh, and  r we still cool?  srry about goin off on u like that this morning.

**Larissa:** yea.

**Cher:** good. Anyway, what was up with u offering that impudent creep 2 sit next 2 u?

**Cher:** hello?

Raul was having trouble typing. Big fingers; small keys.

Mike and Andre were making fun of him as his stubby little fingers pathetically struggled to punch in the words.

"Dang, Raul," Andre whispered. "You're a slow texter!"

"Dude," chuckled Mike, "my grandmother can go faster than that on the freeway!"

Raul slapped Mike's arm.  "Shut up, man! If you think it's that easy, why don't you do it?"

Mike grabbed the phone from him. "Don't mind if I do!"

Raul scoffed. "I'm sure you would. It's not every day you get to talk to a hot girl like Cher . . . or any girl for that matter!"

"Cool it, man! I got a girl!"

"Who," asked Raul. "You mean that big chick that hangs out at the McDonalds every day?"

"Oh yea," Andre remembered. "She's the one always sitting on the bench, eating a Big Mac! That's why we call her 'Biggie Mac' get it? Like Bernie Mac, only with 'Biggie!" Both him and Raul high fived each other.

"Nice one, man!"

Mike blushed. "She got a name."

"Which is . . .?" Raul inquired.

"Bernice."

Raul chuckled, nearly causing him to fall down to the ground. "Bernice! How she come up with a name like that?"

"Her mama, fool!"

Raul shut himself up and ignored him. That's the last we'll be hearing from him.

Mike replied to Cher's text message.

**Larissa:** my bad! I thought Mr. Professa was
watching.

Raul was reading over Mike's shoulder. He slapped his
shoulder after he hit Send. "What are you doing, man?
You'll give away your identity!"

"How?"

Raul pointed at the screen. "You typed Professa," he
said. "Larissa doesn't talk like that!"

"Oh yeah! I forgot!" Raul let out a frustrated groan
and snatched the phone back from him.

"Gimme that before you do somethin' terrible!"

**Cher:** *sarcastically* nice accent.

**Larissa:** uh . . . thx. I thought it was kind of cool. I
learned it from Raul. He's really hot!

**Cher:** r u serious? He's such a freak! I can't believe u
even talked 2 him and his loser friends! And
besides, he can't even rap!

Raul was shocked. He was used to Cher criticizing
his "gangsta" wardrobe, his appearance, and his ghetto
accent. But when he heard Cher insulting his rap skills,
he grew enraged! *Oh, no she didn't!*

Oh, yes she did!

*That's it! Larissa can fight her own battle!* He then
yanked out a piece of paper from his notebook, crumbled
it up into a ball, and then threw it, aiming for Larissa

but somehow hitting Stella instead. She twisted around in her seat.

"Can you stop throwing things," she asked softly. "It's really hard for me to concentrate!"

Raul ignored her whining. "Yeah! Yeah! Whatever! Anyway, do you mind giving this back to Larissa?"

Stella nodded. "Sure."

Raul smiled. "Gracias, chica," he replied in a low, sensual Spanish accent. Raul then sat back in his seat, and for once in his life, he was paying attention.

Stella was about to hand it over to Larissa, but she caught a glimpse of the pink diamonds that decorated her phone. It was so exquisite and tastefully done. *Well, I am curious about what they were talking about in their conversations. Plus, I can probably get some* major *dirt on Cher!* She began searching through Larissa's text messaging history.

Meanwhile, Cher was getting annoyed again. "What's up with that," she spat.

Brittany peered down at Cher. "What is it now?"

"Larissa suddenly stopped texting me!"

"Is she ignoring you *again*?"

"I don't know." *But I'm going to find out!* Cher added in her head. She glimpsed over at Larissa, who was writing stuff in her notebook, but she did find something surprising—Stella Kirkpatrick fiddling around with

Larissa's phone! Cher was so shocked she couldn't keep her gaze off her. *Could she be the one I was talking with all along? This means she knows I insulted her . . .*

Which we all know didn't really bother her. She'd insulted more people worse than she had insulted Stella.

*She likes rap, she obviously doesn't know how to speak English correctly, and she has a thing for Raul! I can really use this to my advantage!* She drummed her fingers on Brittany's desk until she got her attention.

Brittany spun around to face her. "What's up?" she asked.

"Do you know who is in charge of the new student news channel starting, like, next week or somthing? I'm pretty sure they said something about it before school let out last year."

"Isn't that Nadine Potter?" Nadine Potter was definitely a dork around school. Her outfits every day looked like something stolen out of Pippi Longstocking's closet. Her hair was always in eccentric, out-of-this-world styles (for example, she would create two separate pigtails and braid them at the bottom), and she owned bigger wide-rimmed glasses than Steve Urkel, and she wore them every day.

"I heard it starts tomorrow at noon, sharp!" Brittany added.

Cher smiled her signature devilish grin. "Perfect," she glared over at Stella with an evil look in her eye. "Today we prance; tomorrow we pounce!"

The bell rang. Mr. Lance turned around to face the class. "Class, you have no homework for today!" he called out. The class began to holler. "Settle down! Settle down!" he commanded, and they listened. "Just be prepared to work hard tomorrow!"

"Aw come on, Professa Lance," Mike called out. "Go easy on us the first week of school, please?"

"I'm sorry Mr. Jones, but this is how I've planned it out, so it must be followed." Then the students let out groans.

"Whatever," Cher muttered. *I'll just bribe one of the nerds to do my homework for me! I get an A all the time!* Cher picked up her things and waited for Brittany to catch up.

"Why do we have to get hard work the first week back?" Brittany whined as she picked up her tote bag and hung it from her shoulder. The girls walked side by side out of the room.

"Don't even sweat it," Cher assured her. She then leaned in closer so no one else could hear their conversation. "Besides, I can bribe one of the nerds around school to do our homework for us."

Brittany grinned. "You are so smart!"

Sure . . .

"I know! That's why I thought of it!" The two girls smiled and then continued down the hallway toward their lockers.

Stella, who was jamming her books into her messenger bag, was really angry at Cher and Brittany at the moment. *Why would they humiliate me like that in front of all those people? Did I wrong them? Oh yeah, I insulted Cher! So maybe I deserved some of it, but she didn't have to go that far!*

She grabbed her medication off the desk, but instead of putting it away, she stared at it. *And my medication! How could she lie and announce to everyone I'm on depressants? I don't even take drugs! I never have and I never will! Who knows? Maybe she's on drugs?* She plopped her medicine in. She was just about to leave the classroom when she ran into Larissa by the door.

"Hey," Larissa said.

"Hi," Stella replied flatly.

"Need help?" Larissa offered. "You know, finding your locker and everything."

Stella shook her head. "I'm fine, but thanks." She reached into her jean pocket. "Here's your phone, by the way. Raul handed it to me earlier, and I promised to give it back to you."

Larissa took it from her and set it into her purse. "Thanks." She smiled.

Stella suspected she wanted to say something else because she just stood there, staring down at her heels, but she remained silent. "Is there something else you wanted to tell me?"

Larissa let out a deep sigh and looked back up from her shoes. "Look, I'm sorry about what Cher did to you earlier," she said. "She always does things like this to the new people, so don't take it personally."

Stella smiled. *At least she had the decency to apologize . . . even though she didn't do anything.* "It's cool. I mean it's not like you were a part of it." She began to walk toward the door. Larissa followed beside her. The girls began walking side by side down the hall. There were some snickers as Stella exited the class, but the duo did their best to ignore them.

"But I don't understand," Larissa said to her. "How could you just stand there and let her do that to you?"

Stella shrugged. "What was I going to do?"

"Walk away, tell her off, or at least not let her push you around like that."

"It sounds easy, but it's not easy when you actually do it."

Larissa was a little puzzled. "Um . . .?"

"My point is if I walked away she would start mocking me and calling me 'chicken' or 'fraidy cat.'" Larissa was still a little confused, and Stella took notice. "Never mind. You have to be in my shoes to understand."

Larissa shrugged. "So what are you going to do now?"

"Try to ignore her and make new friends." She stopped short and looked down at her feet. "But after that show she put on today, I doubt anyone would want to even come near me now."

Larissa stared at Stella for a while. *Wow! I didn't realize how bad Cher made her feel. I mean, I know Cher made her feel embarrassed, but I didn't think it made her self-esteem go down too!* Stella began walking toward her locker again. Larissa snapped out of her thoughts and followed her.

She finally caught up with her as she was stuffing her textbooks into her floor-length locker. As she was turning the corner, Larissa spotted a couple strolling up to her. The girl stopped next to Stella, while the guy she was with waited patiently by the water fountain. Larissa decided to hide around the corner and watch. *Maybe Stella was wrong. She can make new friends despite the fact Cher hurt her social status!*

********

"Hey, you're the new girl, right?" the girl asked.

Stella had her History book in her grasp. She turned to the girl behind her and nodded. "Yes, why?"

The girl stuck out her hand. "I'm Whitney," she said.

Stella shook her hand. "Stella."

"Cute name."

"It's okay once you get used to it," Stella smiled.

Whitney laughed. "Wow. No one said you had such a great sense of humor."

"I try."

Whitney giggled again.

Meanwhile, Larissa was still spying from the corner. *Yes! Stella is on her way to having more friends and soon causing Cher to lose her power!* Suddenly, she felt someone tap her lightly on her shoulder. She jumped and whipped around to see who it was.

"Expecting someone," Cher asked. She was holding her cell phone while her tote was strung on her shoulder.

"No," Larissa answered quickly. *If I keep my answers short and to the point, she won't ask any further questions.*

"Okay," Cher replied, not too convinced Larissa was telling her the truth. "What are you looking at then?" Larissa opened her mouth to say something, but Cher didn't even bother to wait for an answer. She brushed Larissa to the side and peeked around the corner and then quickly turned back, smiling widely.

"Why are you smiling," Larissa asked.

"The girl I hired is here!"

"Why would you hire someone to be nice to Stella?"

"Be nice? Get real! This is just for my own enjoyment!"

Larissa stared at Cher for a moment in complete astonishment. "But why do you enjoy seeing other people get hurt?"

"Because it's fun, duh!"

"But—"

Cher cut her off. "Just drop it and watch!"

Although Larissa wanted to tell her off, she obeyed Cher's commands, as usual.   She sighed. *I'm such a doormat!*

Whitney and Stella were still having a general conversation.

"So you're from New York, right?" Whitney wanted to make sure.

"Yeah, born and raised," Stella told her proudly.

"Cool! I grew up in Chicago, but then I had to move out here when my parents divorced."

Stella froze, unsure how to respond to that bit of news. "Sorry to hear about that."

"It's cool. I mean, I was kind of glad when they broke up."

"Really, why?"

"My dad was a drug addict . . . kind of like you!"

Stella was so shocked after she heard that, her mouth was unable to close. *Oh God! She did* not *just say that to my face!* She and the guy she came with left her while they laughed the whole way down the hall. *Is the whole school out to humiliate me or what!* Stella slammed the locker door shut. Things at Cornelius weren't going the way she had hoped.

Whitney and her boyfriend, Leonard, walked around the corner where Cher and Larissa were waiting. Cher ran up to her to congratulate her on the job.

"That was so good! I can't believe it! She bought your every word!"

"That's why I'm in drama club," she joked. Cher didn't find it funny at all.

"Anyway, can we please get to the next step of my job?" Whitney rubbed her fingers together.

"Oh right! How could I forget? You totally deserve it!" Cher glanced around to make sure the coast was clear before reaching into her purse and pulling out a crisp twenty-dollar bill.

Larissa was stunned when she saw Cher slip it into Whitney's hands. *Bribery? So that's what Cher has resorted to now?*

"Thanks, Cher. Hope to do business with you soon."

"Me too," Cher lied, flashing a fake smile, which was also one of her specialties!

Whitney and Leonard walked down the hall toward their lockers to grab their books for their next class. As soon as Whitney had left, Cher rolled her eyes and turned to Larissa.

"That's a relief! She is such a loser! I can't stand the drama club! Plus, her breath reeked of coffee!"

Larissa wasn't in the mood to hear Cher's insults. "Cher, how could you bribe someone do to something so cruel?"

She shrugged her shoulders. "Easy. I get what I want, so if I want Stella to be humiliated, it has to be done!"

Larissa was disgusted. *How can Cher be so careless toward someone else's feelings? Is it possible for someone to be so inhumane?* "Just because you're spoiled doesn't mean you have to get what you want all the time!"

"Sure it does! I'm popular remember? Everyone at this school wants to be me! I even have a group of wannabe ninth graders worshipping at my feet!"

Larissa glared at her and shook her head in disbelief. "That doesn't mean anything! And how do you even know you're popular?"

Cher was stunned by the question. *That's a stupid question!* she thought. "You really want to know?"

"Yeah, I want to know!"

"I'll show you." She turned and pointed around the whole hallway. Students were still chatting among their friends or texting on their cell phones while others were hurrying back to their classes before the bell rang. And of course, the clones were nearby, pretending to check their makeup in their compacts (though they were actually spying on Cher through their compact mirrors).

She turned back to Larissa. Her eyebrow was raised. "See what I mean?"

"I don't understand."

"These people adore me! They do whatever I tell them! I'm like their den mother." Cher inched closer to Larissa's face. "So when I say don't talk to the new kid, they keep their distance from her! Now do you understand why I'm popular?"

Larissa kept her gaze on Cher's face. "Not really."

"Basically, I was born to be number one, and no one else can take that away from me. Not even your stupid friend, Stella!"

*That's what you think.* Larissa added in her mind. "Oh I understand!" Larissa picked up her tote bag. "See you around." She strutted away toward her locker.

Cher watched as she walked away. *What is up with her lately? It seems like yesterday we were so tight; now she's dissing me?* Cher paused for a moment. *Unless . . . this is a way for her to become friends with Stella! No way! No way is that happening for as long as I'm head of this school!* She then pulled out her cell phone, which was resting in her purse, and speed-dialed Brittany. She walked toward her locker while she waited for her to answer. She was sent to voicemail.

"Hey! This is Brittany! Leave me your name, number, and a cool message and I'll get back to you!"—there was a momentary pause—"Unless you're my ex-boyfriend . . . hang up, Brent, if it's you!" Then there was a beep, and Cher left her message.

"Hey, Britt, it's me, Cher. Listen! I need your help thinking up a plan to keep Stella away from Larissa. Anyway, we'll talk it over at lunch. Kisses!" Cher hung up and slipped her phone back into her purse. *If this is the way Stella wants it . . . she'll definitely get it that way!* She made it to her locker, got her World Civ book out, and left for her class.

**Stella and her crushed spirits: -2 points.**

**Cher and her plan for mass destruction: 7 points.**

# 7

Larissa had just gotten done with her Spanish 1 class and was making a mad dash to her locker, trying to avoid Cher at all costs. Once she was able to stash her book in her locker, she fixed herself up a bit and then went around searching for Stella. *I hope I don't find Cher along the way!* Luckily, she didn't!

She did find Stella talking with Gia, Tara, and Jade at Tara's locker. Just before she was about to walk up to them, Larissa made a mental note: *Remember, you want to be friends with the new girl, so whatever you do, don't lose your cool, and be friendly!* She smoothed out the creases in her skirt, straightened up her posture, and then casually walked up to the girls. "Hey," she said cheerfully.

They all turned to see who was greeting them. When they saw it was Larissa, Gia rolled her eyes while Tara and Jade let out disgusted groans.

Stella, on the other hand, was actually rather astounded. "You again," she asked.

Larissa forced a smile. *Is she mad because I came to check on her?* "Yeah, it's me," she replied. "I was just checking if you were still upset about earlier."

"As you can see, she's fine," snapped Tara, "so if you don't mind, we would like for you to leave now! We were in the middle of a conversation before you rudely disrupted us!"

Larissa wanted to tell her off, but she remembered her mental note, so instead she calmly answered by saying, "Don't worry. I'm not here to interrupt."

"Good. Then leave," Jade retorted.

"Can I at least finish?"

"No, you can—" Gia started to say, but Stella cut her off mid-sentence.

"Guys, let her finish." She signaled to Larissa for her to continue.

Larissa smiled with gratitude, but Stella didn't bother to make any friendly gesture back to her. "I actually wanted to invite you guys to eat lunch with me today."

Tara raised her blonde eyebrow. "Lunch? With you," she asked, confused by Larissa's sudden invitation. As you've probably guessed, they hardly got invited to anything.

"Yeah, why not?"

"Well, I hate to be bearer of bad news," started Gia, "but you and your friends hate us!"

"Correction: *Cher* hates you, not me."

"Then why do you always insult us or make fun of the things we do every time you're around her?"

Larissa paused. She knew the answer to that question.

Larissa remembered back to the ninth grade when Cher so desperately wanted to be popular.

Let's just say junior high wasn't the best years of her life.

She told Larissa to hate everyone at school and to only associate with the select few (the cool kids). Sadly, Larissa obeyed Cher's wishes. So now she had to create a friendship out of scratch with the surfer chicks.

"It's a long story," Larissa said, avoiding getting into detail. "All I know is I want to make it up to you guys."

Gia gestured to her friends to huddle up. They did, and almost immediately began discussing. "Should we let her in?" Gia whispered.

"I don't know. What if she's doing Cher's dirty work by going undercover?" Jade asked.

"I doubt it! She seemed really nice to me when we were talking on the way to our second periods," Stella added. "In fact, I think she wants to help us!"

"That's all a part of her cover!" Tara loudly whispered.

"I'm with Tara. What if she really is doing Cher's dirty work?" Gia asked. "You can't trust a lot of people around here, especially a best friend of Cher's."

"I don't think she's like that," Stella stated. The others sighed. "Come on, guys; give her a chance. Please!" Stella gave them her sad eyes.

"No! Not the sad eyes!" Tara softly shouted. The other girls giggled.

"Fine! But if she disappoints us once, then that's it!" Gia announced.

"Okay." The girls turned back to Larissa.

Gia decided to be their spokesperson. "Since you sound so sincere and not fake, we're giving you a *small* chance to prove yourself."

Larissa was surprised. *They're actually giving me a chance?* "Wow! I can't believe you guys are forgiving me like this."

"Whoa! Nobody said anything about forgiveness," Jade said.

Larissa became a little disappointed, but she accepted their decision. "I understand, but I'll—"

"I was just kidding," She smiled. The girls laughed.

"Let's head over to the cafeteria now. I want to get there before all the seats at Chicke-Dee's are taken."

\*\*\*\*\*\*\*

As usual, the cafeteria was packed. The large orange-and-white-painted room was filled with unruly children who were talking and joking around with their friends at various restaurants.

That was because that was one of the only places on campus where no teacher would ever be found.

"Can it be any louder in here," Stella shouted.

"What," Larissa shouted back.

"I said . . . can it be any louder in here!"

"Tell me later!" Stella rolled her eyes. *What's the point? You'll probably be deaf by the time we get to wherever we're going!*

The girls casually walked over to Café Renee. Larissa kept a lookout for Cher. She was nowhere in sight, which was a good thing. *At least we can eat our lunches in peace,* she thought. Because if Cher found Stella and the surfer chicks eating in a spot she had reserved for the rich and popular only, Larissa, Gia, Stella, Jade, and Tara would all be banished to eat near the garbage cans for the rest of their high school years, which was worse than the Chicke-Dee's punishment.

When they reached the café, Larissa hadn't seen a trace of Brittany or the rest of Cher's friends. There were just a couple of people sipping cappuccinos at a large round table. They snickered when they saw Stella walk in. *Why are they laughing?* Stella asked herself. *Do I have toilet paper stuck to my shoe?* She stared down at her shoe. There was nothing there. *Maybe they're laughing at something else?* But they weren't. They kept on staring and laughing at her. *Oh, they're laughing because I'm apparently a drug addict!*

"Hey Stella," one of the boys called out. Stella and her friends glanced over. "You got any cocaine with you? I was planning on getting high after school!" His friends and a couple cheerleaders giggled.

"Just ignore him," Larissa whispered to her. Stella nodded and followed Larissa to a table in the back.

"If you don't have cocaine, how much do you charge for pot," his other friend called out.

"Do you keep them in that ratty old sack you call a backpack?" A brunette cheerleader called out. She had on a skimpy mini dress with stiletto heels. Dark red lipstick was coated all over her lips like a drag queen. She laughed at her own comment.

Tara was really getting annoyed with that obnoxious band of kids. She turned to face them and shouted, "Hey Madison! Did you lease those boobs or borrow them?"

The girl rolled her eyes. "At least I *have* boobs!"

Tara held up her fist. "You want to say that to my face, Skanky Barbie!"

Larissa raced over to Tara to stop the fight. "Girls, that's enough."

"Ooh! Do you want to fight me then?" Madison asked, standing up to ready herself.

Larissa glared over at her. "I don't waste my time with people who aren't my class!" And with that, Larissa led Tara over to their table.

"Thanks for saving me," Tara said once the two girls had sat down.

"No problem," Larissa responded. In the meantime, Jade was admiring the café. It was painted white, gold, and sultry red. *Wow. No wonder the popular kids don't want to share this place! It's beautiful!*

"So this is the sanctuary where the rich and popular eat!" Gia commented as she searched through the menu written in elegant script letters.

"It's really not that great," Larissa muttered.

"It is if you've been sentenced to eat at Chicke-Dee's for the past two years!" Tara exclaimed.

"Shush! Not so loud!" Larissa whispered.

"What's wrong?" Jade asked.

"I don't want people to hear you."

"Oh, so now you're ashamed of us?" Gia asked her with arms folded.

"No! It's not like that. It's just—"

"I thought you wanted to be our friend?" Tara added.

"No! Honestly, I'm not ashamed of you, and I do want to be your friend. It's just that"—she leaned in closer to them to whisper—"I don't want the popular people seeing you."

"Let them!" Jade shouted. "Now they'll know they can't tell us where to eat from now on!"

"Seriously, guys. If Cher—"

"So this is about Cher, right?" Stella asked, disappointed in Larissa's sudden change in behavior.

"No! It's about . . . just forget it." Larissa sat back in her seat, holding her stomach feeling like she might be sick. The other girls looked at her confusingly. *What am I doing? I want them to like me! Okay, Evans, you have to vow to yourself not to bring up Cher or anyone else who is a part of her evil clique . . . wait . . . I'm still a part of her evil clique! Okay, new vow! I'm vowing not to bring up Cher or anyone else trying to sabotage Stella's life! There, that was easy!*

"What do you guys want to eat?" Larissa asked once she had settled down.

"You okay now?" Stella asked.

"Or are you too ashamed to tell us?" Tara remarked.

"I'm fine, and I'm sorry if I made you guys feel unwelcome."

"It's cool," Jade said to her. "Besides, you're paying," she giggled.

Larissa grinned, not minding the idea one bit. "Fine, but you owe me!"

"Deal," Jade beamed.

"Now that that's over," Tara said, "can we order something to eat, please?"

"Yeah, I'm starving!" Stella exclaimed.

"Me too." Larissa said. She picked up a menu and scanned it. "I guess I'll try—"

Just then, a wild group of friends came walking in. Larissa recognized them as her friends . . . including Cher! She quickly lowered her face into her purse.

"What's wrong now," Gia whispered.

"Look up!" Larissa whispered back.

Gia did just that and spotted Cher and her clique of friends. "Oh shoot, Cher's here." She grabbed her menu before looking at all her friends. "Hide behind your menus!" And they did. The girls did their best to remain quiet so they could hear what her friends were ranting about.

"You should've seen it!" Cher exclaimed. "It was completely hilarious! In fact, I should've won an Oscar!"

"What did you do exactly?" Carlos asked. He pulled up a chair and sat backwards on it.

"Well, we insulted her outdated outfit, ridiculed her appearance, and found out she's having some problems."

"Big problems," Brittany added. She had called in earlier to pre-order a mocha latte, and a student who worked there part-time was just delivering it to her.

"Here you go, Brittany."

She glowered at him. "That's Ms. Wellington to you, dirt bag," she scolded.

It was easy to tell she was trying to talk like Cher.

Her friends began laughing at the guy, as he blushed hard. "Sorry. I won't call you Brittany again."

"Good! Now leave my sight!"

"But you haven't paid for your latte."

Brittany rolled her eyes but finally pulled out her American Express credit card. "Charge it," she commanded. The guy left with the card in his hand.

"What a dork," Cher exclaimed.

"He can't even dress properly!" Brittany added as she pointed out his high-rise corduroys. "My five year old cousin has better fashion sense!" He came running back with the card and handed it to her. Brittany snatched it up and placed it into her Coach wallet. He also handed her a receipt and a pen for her to sign.

"Please sign at the bottom." Brittany rolled her eyes and signed her name before shoving both the receipt and the pen back to the guy. He smiled and thanked her.

Once he had left, Mitchell spoke up. "You never told us about Stella's problem."

"Oh yeah! It was the biggest news I've gotten in a while."

Meanwhile, Stella was listening. *Oh no! God, please save me,* she pleaded.

"What was it?" T. J. asked.

"We found drugs in her backpack!" Cher yelled. The gang laughed hysterically. Stella nearly cried as she heard all those people laughing at her expense.

"Drugs! How did you manage to find them?" Mitchell asked.

"They fell out."

"Huh?"

Brittany jumped in. "You won't believe it! She has a hole at the bottom of her backpack!" The crowd laughed even more.

"Hasn't she heard of buying a new one?" Tommy asked.

"She can't. She's poor!" Brittany mocked. "Probably so poor, she forgot what a dollar looked like!" Stella almost cried again but had to suck her tears in before she blew her cover.

"Dude, check this out." T. J. stood up in front of his friends. "Welcome, Cheap R Us shoppers! There's a sale going on right now on cheap school supplies! I repeat there is a sale going on right now on cheap school supplies!" he teased. His friends laughed.

Mitchell joined him. "Buy one backpack, get free drugs inside," he added.

More tears flooded Stella's eyes.

Cher also added to the entertainment. "Do you hate zippers? Well, if you do, we have a more convenient way to get things out of your backpack! Going on now, for a limited time only, cashiers will cut out holes at the bottom of your bag at the time of purchase. Free of charge!"

The gang laughed hysterically. They couldn't contain themselves much longer . . . and neither could Stella.

Stella shot up from her seat and sprinted out of the café.

"Stella, wait!" Tara called out to her. Both Tara and Jade ran after her.

Gia got up too, but waited for Larissa to join her. "Are you coming, Larissa?"

*Shoot! There goes my cover,* thought Larissa.

Cher couldn't believe it. Larissa looked up at her. Cher was glaring at her coldly. Her arms were folded across her white Dolce & Gabbana cap-sleeved blouse, the new top she changed into shortly before lunch.

The reason she was wearing a different outfit was that she had vowed in the ninth grade to wear two outfits every school day. That way all the attention would still be on her and her new outfit.

"Well?" Gia asked again tapping her Vans against the tiled flooring. Larissa slowly stood up, snatched up her handbag off the table, and was about to run out of the cafeteria when Cher called out to her.

"Larissa." Larissa looked back and could see how hurt Cher was by staring deep into her eyes. She let out a sigh and mouthed *I'm sorry.* And with that she followed Gia out of the cafeteria, not even worried about Cher's glare.

Cher stood there, sad and confused. *Stella. If it weren't for Stella, Larissa wouldn't have followed Gia in the first place! She'd be here, where she belongs!* She glanced over at the cafeteria entrance, where she spotted Larissa jogging out. *That Stella girl will definitely pay! If she thinks she can steal my best friend just like that, she has another think coming!*

Cher turned to face her newest companion. "Britt."

"Yeah?"

"Did you get my voicemail from this morning?"

Brittany nodded. "Yeah, about that. What is it exactly you want me to do?"

"Nothing you can't handle."

\*\*\*\*\*\*\*\*

Larissa and Gia found Stella crying hysterically in a stall in the girls' bathroom. Tara and Jade were surrounding her, trying to cheer her up, but it didn't seem like it was working. Larissa and Gia joined them inside. It became a little cramped, but they didn't complain. They figured complaining would only make Stella feel worse.

Larissa was the first to talk. "Stella, I'm so sorry you have to go through all this. It's only your first day, and it's not fair."

Stella glanced up at her from her cupped hands. Her eyes and nose were bright red. "It's okay. It's not your fault." She narrowed her eyes at nothing in particular. "It's that evil witch's fault!" She ripped off another piece of toilet paper and blew her nose.

"I wish there was some way to teach Cher a lesson!" Gia exclaimed. She pounded her fist into her hand repeatedly. "Something she'll surely regret!"

"Maybe we should slash her tires?" Tara suggested. The girls giggled.

"That would be cool, but she gets chauffeured, or she carpools with me," Larissa stated.

"Man," Jade snapped her fingers together.

"That sucks for you!" Tara added. "I'm sure all you ever hear is *my hair is totally awesome*," she squealed in a high-pitched, girly tone.

The girls giggled some more.

"How about we replace her shampoo with shaving cream during gym class!" Jade said. All the girls laughed except for Stella. She didn't want to fight any longer. She had had enough already!

"Guys, what's the point? She'll just come back around and do something even worse!" Stella croaked.

"So what? She's been torturing you like crazy . . . and it's only the first day!"

"I know, but I really don't want to fight back until it's really necessary."

"You aren't quitting, are you?" Gia asked.

"No," Stella stood up, "I'm just waiting until the time is right." She stroked her forehead gently. "Besides, I already have a massive headache from today's events."

Larissa thought for a moment. *I wonder if shopping will help clear her mind. It helps me when I'm down.*

"I know! Why don't we go shopping?" Larissa suggested.

"That sounds fun!" Jade exclaimed.

Stella shrugged. "I guess."

"Great! You all can come over my house after school to talk more about this. Deal?"

"Us? Going to *your* house?" Tara asked.

"Yeah…" Then Larissa had to quickly shut herself up. She had realized it was not every day these girls got the invitation to go home with a popular girl like herself.

"Sure," Tara answered. "When should we meet you there?"

"The same time I'll be there! You'll be coming with me in my car."

Stella was starting to clear up now. "And what car are we talking about," she asked.

"Is it that important?"

"Just curious."

"Okay. It's a Mercedes-Benz. No big deal!"

Gia, Tara, Stella, and Jade all squealed. Larissa shushed them. "Quiet down! Don't turn this into a riot!"

"Sorry, but it's not like I get to ride in a Mercedes every day!" Stella shouted. "Or any expensive car, for that matter!"

"Well, there's a first time for everything!"

"I can't wait!" Tara exclaimed.

Gia checked her watch. "We'd better leave before the afternoon rush gets in here," she said. "I saw a lot of people eating at Giovanni's Pizza Parlor, if you know what I mean." The girls cringed when Gia said that. They knew what that meant.

Jade cringed. "Sadly, I know what that means too!"

"Yeah, let's get out of here!" Stella announced. "The last thing I need is to hear fart noises."

"And smelling it," Larissa added. The girls laughed as they piled out of the crammed stall. They left the bathroom and headed back to get to their classes on time.

**Cher and Brittany: 2 points.**

**Stella and her friends' support: 6 points.**

# 8

Cher sat at a desk in the back. That was a place Cher had reserved just for her and her friends Mitchell, T. J., and Brittany, who were sitting nearby, as always.

"So how are we going to do this?" Brittany asked Cher as she pulled out her English textbook. "It's not going to be easy,"

Cher scoffed. There was hardly anything impossible for Cher . . . unless you count being nice.

"There is *nothing* impossible for me!" Cher blurted. "Just know it'll be done!" She used her finger to tap the side of her head. "It's all up here."

"If you say so," Brittany said with a sigh, "but what if it doesn't work?"

Cher rolled her eyes. "Stop questioning me and, for once, trust me!"

Brittany raised her hands up, surrendering. "Sorry! It won't happen again!"

"Good."

Just then, the wooden door was flung open and Larissa stepped in.

"Well! Well! Well! If it isn't Ms. Backstabber herself!" Brittany shouted out. Larissa was busy looking around for a place to sit.

Cher glanced at her. *Why, Larissa? Why did you ditch me for that other chick? I thought we were friends?*

Not when you boss her around like Donald Trump!

*Maybe if I offer to let her sit next to us, she'll know I'm not mad at her and she'll be my best friend again so I can dump Brittany back down to her original status of a lame and obnoxious field hockey tramp! I just hope Larissa will say yes.*

Larissa finally found a seat up front. She knew Cher took this class, which meant she sat in the back with Mitchell, T. J., and now Brittany. *Please don't let her see me!* Larissa was trying to power-walk over to the empty desk, but unluckily for her anyway, Cher spotted her.

"Larissa," she called out.

Larissa glanced over and saw Cher gesturing for her to come over. She rolled her eyes. *What does she want now? Doesn't she realize I'm trying to be alone . . . and avoid her!*

*What?* Larissa mouthed to her. Cher wouldn't leave her alone. She signaled to Larissa to come over to her, this time with more aggression.

After being reluctant for quite some time, Larissa finally walked up to her. "Yeah," she asked rudely.

"Aren't you sitting with us?" Brittany inquired, pointing at the other empty desk next to her. "There's a desk sitting right here with your name on it."

Larissa replied by saying, "Actually, I was thinking about—"

Cher cut her off. "This isn't an invitation. It's an order, so do it!" Cher and Larissa glowered at each other for a while.

*This is your chance! Tell Cher how you really feel,* thought Larissa. "Well that's an order I just can't follow!" And after that was all said and done, Larissa stormed up to the front of the class and sat down at the desk she had picked earlier.

"This is going way too far!" Cher bellowed once Larissa had stomped away. "Who does she think she is?"

"Don't sweat it, Cher." Mitchell assured her. "She'll come back to her senses soon."

But Cher wasn't being calmed down by Mitchell's words. "Well I can't wait that long!" She glared at Larissa once more. "She'd better realize who her real friends are before I do it for her!"

# 9

"This car is so cool!" Stella exclaimed. She admired all the cool features in the car, such as the TV and the fridge.

"What does this button do," Tara asked. She pressed it, and before she knew it, the sunroof glided open.

"Sweet," Gia hollered. All the girls, except for Larissa, stuck their heads out the sunroof and began shouting random stuff at the students who were walking to their cars.

Larissa was busy looking outside the window, distracted by her own problems. *Should I really betray Cher like this? I mean, we're best friends! We've been best friends since kindergarten!* She stole a peek at Stella, who was chatting with her other friends. She seemed so happy. *But then again, she's hurting Stella for no other reason than that she was the new girl!* The sound of the car door closing brought her back down to earth.

"Sit down and buckle up, everyone!" Sam ordered. The girls obeyed.

Gia leaned in closer to Larissa. "You even have a driver?" Gia asked enviously.

"Guilty!"

"I officially hate you," she joked. The girls giggled. He then started the car and pulled out of the school grounds.

They had been on the road for about four minutes when Stella thought, *Well, I wasn't able to get any dirt on Cher today from Larissa's cell phone. There has to be another alternative. But who or what?* She quickly looked over at Larissa, who was reapplying her lip gloss as she gazed at her reflection in her compact mirror. A smile spread across Stella's face.

We all know what that means . . .

"Hey, Larissa," Stella, who was now browsing through the refrigerator, called out.

Larissa looked up from her compact. "Yeah?"

"Was there ever a time when Cher was actually . . . nice?"

Gia, Tara, and Jade, who were talking among themselves, burst out laughing.

"Stella, let's be rational here!" Gia guffawed. "There is *no* possible way that Wicked Witch of the West was a

141

kindhearted person!" That was a secret nickname people (i.e. losers) at school had given her.

"I bet she was a terror even when she was a baby," added Tara, "like beheading her Barbie dolls because their eye shadow wasn't the 'perfect shade of blue'!" The girls chortled some more.

"I agree! Cher being nice is like Yao Ming being short!" Jade joked. All the girls laughed except Larissa.

"Who's Yao Ming," she asked stupidly. The three girls stared at her blankly.

"Are you serious," Tara asked.

"Duh!"

"You don't know who Yao Ming is," Gia asked.

"Nope!"

"I'm not a sports kind of person either," Jade said, "but even I know who he is!"

"So is anyone going to tell me who he is or not?"

"All right! All right! He's a 7' 6" basketball player for the Houston Rockets," Gia said.

"Wow! He must be really good if he's that enormous!"

"Yeah"—Jade paused—"At least I think he is?"

"Trust me," said Tara, "he is!"

Stella asked her question again, seeing her friends were getting off course—something they tended to do. "But seriously . . . what was she like before?"

Larissa paused for a moment, reminiscing about all the sleepovers and fun times they used to share. "The best friend a girl could ever ask for."

The others snickered. Even Sam chuckled to himself, but none of the girls heard him anyway.

"You guys, I'm being serious." They stopped and stared at her.

"Really? You mean she actually acted more like a human being than a devil in disguise!"

"I know it's hard to believe, but she was much sweeter back then."

"Boy, do I wish I knew her then!" Gia proclaimed.

"You would've loved her. We had the most amazing times together!"

"What did you guys do?" Stella asked.

"What all girls do: we went shopping, got our nails done, had sleepovers, and tons of other girly stuff!"

"What about her personality?"

"She was sweet and really caring. She really loved her family and friends, especially her mom. But . . ."

"But what? Tell us what happened!" Tara begged. (She was good at that kind of stuff.)

"Promise you won't tell anyone, especially Cher." The girls held out their pinkies and linked them together in a circle.

"Pinkie swear," Jade shouted. They unlinked pinkies. Larissa took a deep breath and then began.

"Okay. This is a little complicated, so pay attention."

"Yeah, got it! Got it! Got it! Just get on with the story!" Tara blurted out. (Then there were those times she was really annoying.)

Gia slapped Tara's arm. "Shut up! She can't tell the story if you're screaming in her face!"

Tara frowned. "Sorry, Mother," she joked. The other girls laughed. Gia rolled her eyes at Tara's immaturity.

"Anyway, Cher's family and my family used to live in New York."

"No lie?" Stella exclaimed.

"No lie."

"Who cares? Just finish the story!"

This time all the girls shouted, "Tara!"

"Sorry."

They rolled their eyes but giggled.

"Back to the story . . . and this time no interruptions!" Larissa specifically gazed over at Tara.

"I got it! I got it!"

The girls giggled some more.

"Okay . . . back in New York, Cher lived with her parents. They seemed like the perfect family. Mr. and Mrs. von Seaton were always together, nonstop! It made Cher sick sometimes, but she somehow liked the fact they weren't arguing. Well, the years went on, and we were just about to graduate from eighth grade when Cher's family life began changing. Her parents couldn't stop fighting."

"Why were they fighting?" Jade asked.

"According to Cher, her mom thought her dad's computer software business would never become a success. He was trying to make it grow at the time. She used to come to my house every night, crying. Cher, that is. I remember her telling me that she could hear her parents arguing at night up in her room over bills, payments, and even Cher's school tuition. Then, before she knew it, her dad had left."

"Her dad left?" Gia asked.

"Don't worry; he came back."

"How long was he gone?" Jade asked.

"About five months."

"Wow!"

"Yeah. Anyway, her family went back to being happy. Mr. and Mrs. von Seaton worked out their differences so the family wouldn't have to go through those changes again."

"So are they okay now?" Stella wanted to know.

"Well, sort of . . ."

"What do you mean?"

"It was May thirteenth, two thousand and four. We were walking home from school. I had just dropped her off at her house. A few minutes later, she ran back to my front yard."

"What happened?" Tara asked anxiously.

"She told me she found her mother in bed with another man!" All three girls' eyes widened.

"Shut up! Her mom slept with another guy?" Gia asked.

"Sadly, yes."

"She must've been heartbroken." Stella stated.

"She was. She couldn't eat for weeks. Her doctors told her she was losing about two pounds a day!"

"How did she survive?" Tara asked.

"She drank stuff and nibbled on snacks, but that's about it."

"How did her dad take it?"

"That's a different story!"

"Tell us," Gia urged.

"Okay. After Cher found her mom in bed, her mom had gone into hiding at the man's house for a couple weeks. Over those weeks, Mr. von Seaton drank a lot. He was so depressed. Poor Cher had to watch her dad suffer. His doctors told him if he hadn't been careful, he would've died because of alcohol overdose and liver malfunction."

"Whoa!"

"Yeah! It was pretty serious. So when her mom came back, Mr. von Seaton had already packed her bags. They were thrown out onto the front yard carelessly. He told Cher to go over my house because it was probably going to get ugly. So Cher came over and we watched from my yard. Her mom came in the afternoon and met him on the stoop, where he was finishing up a bottle of Jack Daniels. He yelled, 'Leave! You good-for-nothing heartbreaker! Go be with your real man, 'cause he's not here!' Cher's mom pleaded with him, but he threatened to bash her head with the whiskey bottle, so she grabbed her bags and left."

"What about Cher?" Tara asked. "How did she take it when she saw her mom leave like that?"

"Of course she was devastated, but at the same time, she was disappointed in her mother. I mean, think about it. Would you want your mom cheating on your dad?"

Tara and Jade shook their heads, but Gia remained silent. The truth was that her dad had left her family on her fifteenth birthday. She remembered sitting on the beach; all her friends and family were there to celebrate with her. But when she saw her mom run down from their old house, holding a note and crying, Gia knew that from that point on, her father would never come back.

"So what about Cher's family now," she heard Stella ask.

"Well, Mr. von Seaton's company grew into one of the biggest software companies in the world! Now, Cher's an heiress to about $200 million dollars!"

"No wonder she acts like a spoiled brat!"

"Now she is. I think it might be because her dad got remarried."

Tara shot up. "There's more to the story?"

"If you calm down, I'll tell you."

Tara sat up straight and pretended to zip her lip. "Mum's the word."

"Okay. The summer before she went into ninth grade, her father made a killing with his software, so he bought a fifteen-million-dollar estate in Mavis Gardens and moved out here with Cher. She was so happy to live in a new place at first . . . but she had no idea her dad was going to find a new romance too."

"So, did Cher like her new step mom?"

"Cher? No way! Cher hates her. She wasn't ready for a new mother . . . not after what happened the last time. Plus, she convinced herself her stepmother was a gold digger."

"Typical Cher! Always accusing people of being something so she'll have a reason to hate them!" Gia exclaimed. The girls giggled.

"Isn't that the truth," Larissa chuckled.

"Like Cher would say, 'Duh!'" Tara mocked. The girls laughed even more.

"We're here," Sam announced. The girls looked up. They marveled at the wide property as Sam maneuvered his way up the long private drive. Finally, they pulled up into the courtyard.

The Evanses' mansion was a white and blue 1950s-style home. It had belonged to a famous Hollywood actress who sold it to Larissa's grandmother back in the 1970s. Sam parked in front of the entrance leading into the house. He exited the car. Gia was about to open the door when Larissa stopped her.

"Gia, don't!"

"Why not?"

"You'll see." Sam opened the door, and Larissa exited the car. The others were amazed.

"Now that's what I call first-class treatment!" Tara proclaimed. The others rolled their eyes. The girls exited the car as well. Sam shut the door and grabbed each of their bags from the trunk.

"Does he need help?" Jade asked Larissa.

"I've tried for years, but he insists it's his 'honor' to carry the load," she replied. Jade shrugged.

Sam reached into his suit pocket and pulled out his key for the house. He unlocked the door and gestured to the girls. "Ladies first." The girls walked in, and Sam followed behind them.

Stella admired the entrance with awe. The front steps were astounding! There was one large staircase that curved its way up to the second floor. A huge crystal chandelier hung from the ceiling, and a big, round cherry table was directly below it with a floral arrangement set on top to perfect the look. It was similar to Cher's foyer.

A short, fairly plump lady came walking in. She greeted the girls with a smile. "Welcome to the Evans estate. My name is Gretchen, the head maid," she said warmly. "If you need anything, you can find me or any of the other maids around the house." Sam handed her their school bags, flashing a smile. Gretchen winked back. Stella noticed. *Is that even normal around here?*

He turned to the girls. "If you'll excuse me, I must take the car in for its annual maintenance checkup."

"Cool. See you in a bit!" Larissa shouted over her shoulder. Sam left the house. Gretchen set the bags in the living room before attending to the girls' needs.

"Is there anything I can help you with now," she asked.

"Can I use your phone?" Gia asked.

"Of course. Follow me." Gia followed Gretchen to the kitchen.

"Wait up," Tara called. She caught up with them. Jade followed. Stella chose not to reach her parents. If anything, her brother Jason was home now, and he was the last person she wanted to talk to.

"Don't you want to call your parents?" Larissa asked.

"Na! They're probably at work anyway."

Larissa shrugged. "If you say so." She grabbed a mint out of her handbag and plopped it into her mouth. She offered one to Stella, but she rejected it.

"I'm not hungry right now."

"Suit yourself." Larissa threw the wrapper into a gold-trimmed trash bin in the elegant living room. "Anyway, want to ditch the others and head up to my room?"

"Won't they get lost?"

"Not with Gretchen. She'll figure out we're in my room and she'll bring them up."

"In that case, let's go."

Larissa's room was, as you know, completely pink! She had pink chairs, a pink alarm clock, pink rugs, pink walls, and even a collection of pink stuffed animals. Larissa walked over to her fuzzy pink saucer chair and pulled off her wedges. She threw them over by her computer desk and slipped into her soft pink slippers.

"Ah," she said once she felt the comfort of them. "It's nice to kick off my painful heels and slip into something comfortable, you know."

Stella was busy gazing around her room to answer. It was so much different from hers. It was a lot bigger, too! *So this is how the rich and famous live?*

Tootsie ran out of her small-canopied dog bed and leaped into Larissa's lap. Larissa began stroking her groomed fur as Tootsie wagged her tail in excitement. She loved it when Larissa came back from school.

Stella walked over to Larissa and her dog. "Can I pet her," she asked.

"Sure." Larissa handed her the puppy.

Tootsie began licking Stella's face, which caused her to giggle. "Stop it," she chortled, but the puppy wasn't showing any signs of stopping. Larissa got up to assist Stella in peeling Tootsie away from her. The puppy jumped back down onto the soft carpet and padded back over to her bed with her tiny paws. Just then, Gia, Tara, and Jade poured into the room.

"Whoa!" Tara shouted out. "This room is awesome!"

"It's like Barbie's magic dream room!" Gia added sarcastically. The day just wouldn't have been complete without her sarcasm.

Larissa rolled her eyes. She loved being rich and owning expensive items, but sometimes it made her feel lonely, as if money was the only thing that people saw about her. That's how Cher got the reputation of being the Wicked Witch of the West. She was mean, snobby, arrogant, backstabbing, and life ruining. Money was the only reason people liked Cher. Larissa didn't want the same thing happening to her.

Jade noticed Larissa's puppy in Stella's arms. "You even have a dog," she exclaimed as she ran up to it. "I love dogs! I've always wanted one!" But when she came up to her, Tootsie growled.

"Why does she hate me," she asked Larissa timidly.

"Maybe she doesn't want to be bothered." Larissa answered. "Sorry if she scared you."

"It's cool," Jade sighed. "I'm used to animals hating me anyway."

Gia rolled her eyes. "You always think animals hate you!"

"Only because it's true!"

"One incident at the zoo and you think *all* animals are out to get you," Tara shouted.

"What happened?" Larissa asked.

"We went to the zoo one year over the summer. It was a great day, and we were all having a blast—until Jade threw a peanut into the monkey's cage. The monkey threw it back at her, so now she's thinks all the animals in the world hate her." The girls began laughing uncontrollably.

Jade felt ashamed. "It's not that funny."

Larissa calmed down. "We're not laughing at you; we're laughing *with* you!"

Jade playfully slapped her arm. "Very funny! Anyway, can we get off this subject and get ready to go shopping?"

After the girls calmed down from their hysteria, Tara said, "Okay. We'll stop making fun of you."

"Thank you!"

"But you have to admit, it was funny," Gia muttered under her breath.

Jade whipped her head around. "I heard that!"

The girls laughed even more and sauntered into Larissa's large walk-in closet. Tootsie ran in after them.

********

"Larissa, you are the luckiest girl I have ever met!" Jade announced. She pulled out a silk camisole and held it up to her upper body.

"You like it?"

"Like? I love it! This is way too sweet!"

Larissa's closet was huge! There were maybe forty to fifty racks filled with camisoles, shirts, blouses, jeans, skirts, and pants. If a person wasn't familiar with the closet, he or she could probably get lost in there!

"This is not a closet," marveled Tara, "it's a frickin' Wal-Mart!"

Gia picked up one of Larissa's pointy black pumps. It was a Marc Jacobs creation with a gold chain along the side. She examined it oddly. "How can you wear these things," she asked, still eyeballing it.

Larissa glanced over. Her face gleamed radiantly. "I've been looking for these shoes for weeks," she announced. "Where did you find it?"

"On the rack." Gia answered, a little confused. "You mean you couldn't find a shoe that was here all along?"

"No. Kind of hard to believe, huh?"

"*Very* hard to believe!" Gia rolled her eyes and continued to give herself a tour of the closet.

"Hey, Larissa," Stella called from the winter clothes section, "if you don't mind, do you think we can borrow some of these clothes to go shopping in?" The 'we' was referring to her, Tara and Jade. Gia opted not to get all dolled up. She felt happiest in her Hawaiian-print shirts and khaki shorts.

"Sure! Help yourself! I have plenty of clothes for everyone."

"Thanks," Tara said.

The three went off to separate parts of the closet and began raiding everything they could lay their hands on.

"What about you, Gia?" Larissa asked when she saw she was staring down at the carpet.

"I'll pass. I'm not really into the big designer names."

Larissa turned to face her. "Are you sure you don't want to at least change into something else?"

"Yeah," she walked over to the exit. "I'll be in the room if you need me." Suddenly, she was starting to hate poverty.

Larissa was a little thrown off by Gia's behavior. *Why is she suddenly acting like she hates being here?* Larissa ignored her thoughts and went back to finding an outfit. *Maybe she's just tired.* She finally found her white baby-doll tube dress and espadrilles to match. She quickly left to go to the bathroom and change.

The girls found Larissa at her vaniy, applying sheer Chanel lip gloss to her lips. Once she was done, she smacked them together, plopped the tube into her purse, and was about to leave the room when she saw her friends behind her.

"Ready to leave," she asked.

"Sure, let's go," Stella replied.

Gia got up from the floor. "Thank you," she said. She opened the door and left the room.

"What's her problem?" Jade whispered.

"I don't know," Larissa said. "I tried asking her before, but she wouldn't tell me."

"Maybe she's PMSing?" Tara shouted loudly, observing Larissa's extensive makeup collection. You could find everything from bronzers to moisturizers on her vanity.

The other three shushed her. "What," she asked.

"Not so loud. She'll know we're talking about her," Stella hissed.

"Oops!" Tara quickly covered her mouth. "My bad."

Stella rolled her eyes.

"Just try and keep your mouth shut more often," Jade added. "Even though that may be a little bit harder for you!" The girls giggled.

Larissa grabbed her oversized Fendi sunglasses off her armoire and placed them on top of her sleek blonde hair. "Anyway, let's go. We'll probably be shopping at Pink Ice, and I want to get there before tourists start to invade the area. I swear they always take good parking spaces!"

Tara didn't seem to hear what Larissa was ranting about. "Pink Ice," she exclaimed, "I heard that store is amazing!"

"Of course it is! That's why we're going!" Larissa let out a giggle. "I mean, where did you think we were going shopping? Some run-down, secondhand shop!" Larissa laughed at her own joke.

"Actually . . ." She didn't bother finishing her sentence, but Larissa knew where it was going. She stopped and glanced over at Tara. She could see the sad expression on her face. *I can't believe I'm acting so snobbish! I'm a Cher wannabe like those stupid clones that keep on following her around! I'm such a terrible person!*

"I—I'm sorry, Tara. If I had known—"

Tara raised her hand to silence Larissa. "Don't worry about it. You didn't know. At least you took the time to realize what you said and had a big enough heart to apologize."

"Does that mean we're still friends?" Tara smiled, and then, without warning, she hugged Larissa. Jade and Stella joined in, forming a large group hug filled with giggling girls.

Larissa knew that meant they were friends. She couldn't believe she wasn't their friend before! They're so much nicer than Cher. Plus, they don't make a big deal out of things like insults she never meant to say in the first place. They were like the friends she never had.

"Oh shoot," Larissa exclaimed and pulled herself away from her friends.

"What," Stella asked.

She ignored her and pressed Office on her intercom. The rest exchanged puzzled looks.

Gia then burst into the room. "What's taking you guys so long," she blurted out. The three girls shushed her.

She was confused and walked up to her friends. "What's going on?"

Jade pointed at Larissa. "Larissa's on the phone."

"Is that what's keeping you guys in here so long?"

"Just be patient," Tara commanded. The four girls were in disbelief. This was coming out of a girl who always demanded things to be done immediately!

Gia rolled her eyes in impatience and reluctantly stood by her friends.

A man picked up the phone after several rings. "Hello," Royce said.

"Hey, daddy, it's Larissa."

"Hi, dear. How are you? I didn't see you when you came in."

"Sorry. I brought some friends over."

"Cher, I presume?"

*Why does he always have to think about Cher every time I say "I brought a friend over"? Cher isn't my only friend! In fact, I don't consider her a friend!* "Uh . . . actually you don't know them."

"Interesting. I'd love to meet them."

"We're coming down soon because we're going shopping so you can meet them. And since we are, can I borrow your credit card?"

159

The girls were amazed, especially Gia. *Why does she get all the glamorous things? Why is she pretty and I'm not? Because of her, all my friends are starting to like her more! I hate being poor! I hate it! I hate it! I hate it!* Gia exclaimed in her thoughts.

"Larissa," said Royce, "we've gone over this before! You are not allowed to use my credit cards until you learn how to spend responsibly."

"But Dad! That incident happened, like, over three months ago! I promise I won't do it again."

Royce was referring to the time Larissa went shopping with Cher, Jenny, and some other popular girls at school. She had told her dad she was only going to buy one pair of shoes and that was it.  He set her spending limit at one thousand dollars. If she went over that budget, she would be grounded and banned from using his credit card.

The rest is pretty obvious!

"Larissa Kate, don't argue with me," he yelled. "I've told you my answer."

"Come on, Dad! How am I supposed to go shopping then?"

"You have two options: get a job or don't go shopping at all!" Larissa gasped. She lived and breathed shopping!

"Dad, you're embarrassing me!"

"I don't care."

"Dad—"

"Tell you what. If you want, I'll have Samson drive you and your friends to the wax museum when he gets back and—"

Larissa cut him off. "Why on Earth would I want to go to a stupid wax museum with my friends?" *If we really were that interested in wax, which we aren't, I would've told them to look at their own earwax!*

"They have some pretty decent things on display there that I'm sure you and your friends will enjoy."

"Dad, we like to see clothes on display, not wax!"

"You're pushing it!"

Larissa let out a disgusted sigh. She glanced over at her friends for some advice. *"What should I do,"* she mouthed to them. They thought for a moment, and then Stella snapped her fingers.

"Strike a bet with him," Stella whispered.

Larissa gave her a thumbs-up. "Dad, you there," she asked.

"Yeah."

"What if I don't go over five hundred dollars"

"How are you going to do that," he joked. "The Larissa I know can't even look at a price tag less than six hundred dollars."

"Just be assured it'll be done. And you know I never go back on a promise." There was a momentary silence between them.

"Well, you are maturing…"

"So, does that mean a yes?" After he let out a deep sigh, he said, "Okay, but only if you keep your word."

"Deal."

"Come downstairs and I'll lend you my Visa."

"Thanks, Dad."

"You're welcome, sweetie." They hung up. Once they were sure he had hung up, the girls shrieked. Larissa ran up to her friends and wrapped Stella in a warm embrace.

"Stella, you are a genius," Larissa commented.

"Thank you! Thank you very much," she said, imitating Elvis Presley's voice.

"And about those five hundred dollars, how will we be able to afford anything there?" Tara asked. "I heard Pink Ice is pretty expen–"

"Can we go," Gia shouted.

"Okay! Okay! We're already gone!" Larissa exclaimed. The girls left Larissa's bedroom and headed downstairs, toward Royce's study.

*********

Mr. Evans's study was decorated tastefully. There were two large french doors leading outside to a mini patio. The walls were painted a deep blue color to match the Pacific Ocean close by, and a brown three-seat leather couch imported from Italy accented the walls. He also had a forty-two-inch plasma television mounted in one of the far corners. Royce's mahogany desk sat in front of the bay window overlooking the coast. Sometimes he went into this room to relieve his stress rather than do his normal law work.

Larissa led the girls inside the office and walked them over to her dad, who was sitting on his executive chair, reading his newspaper.

"Hi," she said. Her dad peered up from his newspaper and smiled. Mr. Evans was lean for his age because he was constantly on diets and exercising with his personal trainer. He had a slightly receding hairline, but he kept that hidden under his custom-made toupee. He also wore bifocals for reading.

"Hello," he peered over at the girls standing next to his daughter. "Are these the friends you were talking about?"

"Yes," she pointed at them and introduced them individually. "This is Gia, Tara, Jade, and Stella. Guys, this is my dad, Mr. Evans."

"It's nice to meet you girls," he stated.

"The pleasure is ours," Tara said.

"So I assume you guys are ready to go shopping now?"

"You guessed right!" Larissa cried. Her dad chuckled and pushed back his chair to pull out his card, which was hidden in his desk drawer. He then handed it to Larissa.

"Remember what I said," he reminded her.

"Don't worry. I won't overdo it."

He smiled. "That's my girl!"

Larissa leaned in and gave her dad a kiss on his cheek. She stuffed the card into her wallet before putting it back into her handbag.

"Well, we're leaving."

"See you soon."

"Okay, but before I forget, can I borrow your car," she asked. "Mine's too small to fit all of us." He quickly grabbed his car keys off the desk and tossed them to her.

"Be careful."

Larissa caught it perfectly. "I will. See you later."

"Bye." The girls left the office and walked toward the entrance.

They entered the courtyard, and there sat her father's silver 2007 Audi A6. The others went on as Tara stopped in her tracks. Her jaw dropped open. "That's your dad's car," she asked in astonishment.

Larissa glanced back at her. "Yeah. Come on!" Larissa chuckled.

Tara ran up to her friends.

"Larissa, you are officially the coolest chick I have ever met," she exclaimed as she entered the back seat of the car. Larissa smiled, and then she started the car and left the estate.

# *10*

Pink Ice was a huge department store off Sunset Boulevard. Its grand opening was last June. Its purpose was to be a place where women and girls could shop and also hang out with their friends. The inside was decorated with pink crystal chandeliers and pink lighting, and the uniforms for the employees were pink and white jersey dresses.

When Larissa discovered the store, she immediately fell in love with it. Not because the interior design was her absolute favorite color, but because the atmosphere was so different! And that's what Larissa was all about. She loved things that were unique in their own way. The best part of the department store was the chocolate shop called Taste Like Heaven. They had the best hot chocolate! In fact, it was voted the number-one chocolate store in Food Choice magazine last year.

Larissa browsed around the MAC makeup counters trying to find a cute shade of blush to add to her already humongous makeup collection.

"Larissa," she heard a voice call out. She crossed her fingers, hoping it wasn't Cher. Cher normally came in around this time to scan the New Arrivals.

Phew! It was Stella.

She walked up to her friend at the Clinque beauty counter. "What's up," she asked.

"Can I talk to you in private," Stella wanted to know. "I really need your help with something."

"Sure. We can head up to the Lounge."

The Lounge was another spot where teens hung out. It was an open space on the third floor where you could see a spectacular view of downtown Los Angeles. The roof was the shape of a dome and made of glass, so not only could you see the beautiful Californian sky, but it also brought in plenty of natural sunlight. There was also a small drink shop if you felt like drinking smoothies instead of coffee at the chocolate shop. The girls rode the elevators up to the third floor.

There were only a few people at the Lounge. Some children that looked to be about thirteen or fourteen were sipping smoothies and gabbing on and on with their friends. They probably came from West Hollywood Middle School after it let out to just hang. Larissa and Stella ordered two drinks before they picked a table to sit at. Larissa made sure it was far away from them. One thing Larissa hated more than Cher was kids who talked loudly, thinking that they were cool and that they ran the place.

When their orders came, Larissa began to speak. "So, what's up?"

Stella used her straw to swirl her Bana-o-rama Shake around in its plastic cup. "I don't know how to say it," she answered, still staring down at her drink.

"Just say it!"

Stella finally gazed up at her. "But it's complicated."

"Talk slowly then."

"Okay. You see at school this morning, when I got lost getting to Literature class, I saw this guy coming out of the bathroom. He is amazingly cute! His name is Chris Tyler."

Larissa thought she had stopped breathing. Stella had a crush on the guy Cher had a crush on? That was beyond major! And what better way to hurt Cher than to encourage it. "He is cute! The school voted him the best-looking male last year in the yearbook."

"No wonder. He's so dreamy!"

"Did you talk to him?"

"Well, yeah. I asked him where the class was, and he helped me. He even walked me to class!"

"That's so sweet of him!"

"I know, but . . ." She caught a glimpse of the busy streets below her. *How do I tell Larissa? Can I trust her? Should I trust her? Maybe I should keep it to myself . . .* Larissa waved her hand in front of Stella's face.

"Hello," she shouted. "Earth to Stella!"

Stella snapped out of her daydream. "Did you say something?"

"No, you were scaring me, though. Why did you space out on me like that?"

"Thinking, I guess."

"About Chris?"

"Yeah. He was so sweet and really fun to talk with."

"What did you guys talk about?"

"Nothing really, but still, when he talks, it's like the whole world stops."

"Sounds to me like you've been bitten by the love bug!"

"I guess I have," Stella announced, her mind drifting off to another world. Larissa could see Stella was in love. Her eyes gleamed, her face glowed, and she smiled brightly.

*This is perfect! Not only can I help Stella get the man of her dreams, but I can also make sure Cher doesn't get him! Then, without the guy, Cher can't possibly be popular anymore! I love how things work out!*

"You know what I think you should do?"

"What," Stella asked, still a little dazed.

"You should ask Chris out to the Rock Fest after-party this weekend! It's the hottest party of the year!"

Stella crash landed back to earth. "What! You can't be serious?"

"I'm dead serious!"

"Larissa, it's not that simple. I can't just walk up to him and ask. What if he laughs at me?"

"Don't think like that! And if he does say no, you'll always have me, Gia, Tara, and Jade to go with."

"I know . . . but it would be nice to go with a guy to a party for a change."

"Then it's settled!" Larissa stood up and chucked her cup into the nearby trash can.

"What's settled?"

"We are going back downstairs to the teen section, picking out a hot outfit, then finally, at school tomorrow, you'll ask him out."

"You don't honestly think this will work, do you?"

"Trust me, Stella. This plan is foolproof!" *Good enough to get even with Cher, that is.*

# *11*

The Kirkpatricks lived in a small, suburban neighborhood near Santa Monica. Larissa had dropped everyone else at their homes, and Stella was the last person on her list. She glanced at the quaint homes with amusement. You would think she'd find them inferior—like someone else we know—but she actually found them quite interesting! She had grown up around mansions and estates practically her whole life. She had never stepped foot into an average community or anything lower than upper class, if you didn't count her years in New York.

"It's this house right here." Stella pointed at a small house with burgundy shutters and an equally small front yard. A green Saturn station wagon and a blue Honda Civic were parked in the driveway, so Larissa parked on the curb instead. She stopped the car and they both climbed out.

Larissa popped the trunk open, and Stella could grab her backpack—they had stopped at Larissa's house on the way——and her paper bag with the Pink Ice logo across the front. Suddenly she stuffed it into her pack.

"What are you doing?" Larissa asked.

"I don't want my mom to start interrogating me about what's inside this bag."

"Whatever." Larissa was too exhausted from that afternoon to care about Stella's home life. Once she was done, she slammed the trunk shut and then led Larissa to the front door. She opened the door and led Larissa in.

"Mom, I'm home!" Stella cried out. She dropped her backpack next to the steps. Larissa stared at it. *Uh . . . where's the maid?* She thought. Larissa was used to dropping her tote bag anywhere and having one of her maids take it up to her room for her, she nearly forgot she was the guest.

"Stella," a voice cheerfully called out from the kitchen. A brunette lady of average height came strolling out to the living room. She took off her apron and threw it on a table nearby. She walked up and gave her daughter a hug.

"Welcome home," she said. Mrs. Kirkpatrick—Amy—caught a glimpse of Larissa. She stuck out her hand to greet her as well. "Hello."

Larissa shook her hand. "Hi, I'm Larissa. I go to school with your daughter now."

"It's very nice to meet you, Larissa."

"Nice to meet you too."

"I'll go bring you some snacks."

"Oh, that won't be necessary, but water would be fine."

Mrs. Kirkpatrick smiled. "Two waters coming right up!" She left the girls and entered the kitchen. The girls sat down on the gray couch to wait for their requests.

********

"Thanks for the water, Mrs. Kirkpatrick," Larissa said as she set the cup down on the coaster that had been placed on the wooden table. Amy sat on a chair nearby.

"No problem," Amy responded. "And on behalf of Mr. Kirkpatrick and me, we would like to thank you for being so nice to Stella on her first day. She was a little bit nervous about going to a new school."

"It was no trouble at all."

Amy smiled. "Was she shy at all today? She has a little problem with that."

********

"Mom!" Stella's cheeks reddened.

Amy chuckled. "Don't be embarrassed, Stella. Everyone gets shy sometimes."

"Yeah, but did you have to say that in front of Larissa?"

"Oh, stop it!"

Stella rolled her eyes. *Mom is so embarrassing!*

"Anyway, what did you guys do today?"

Larissa and Stella both hesitated to answer.

*Well, Mom . . . I met Cher, the most wicked person I have ever met; the students made fun of my clothes; my medication fell out of my backpack; Cher started a rumor that I'm a drug addict; she had her evil friend took a picture of her, me, and my medicine to put on her blog; and some random person came up to me and also joked about my medicine. So now Cher is bent on destroying my life! Wasn't my day wonderful?*

"We basically had class, ate lunch, and now we're here," Larissa summarized. Stella was shocked. Larissa handled it better than she had expected.

"Sounds like you had a great day."

"Yeah, Mom . . . the greatest," Stella mumbled. She grabbed her infamous backpack. "Well, Mom, Larissa and I are going up to my room now."

"Have fun." She arose from the chair she was sitting at. As she was walking into the kitchen, she called out, saying, "Call me if you need anything!"

"Okay!" Stella called back. Stella led Larissa up the creaky wooden stairs.

They walked down the hall until they got to the second door on the left. Larissa noticed a black sign that read "Enter at your own risk or live to regret it" in big red letters. There were skulls plastered all around the message.

"I assume this is your room?" Larissa asked as she stared at the sign in terror.

"Yep!" Stella answered while she unlocked the door.

*I hope there isn't anything creepy in there too, like fish eyes!* Larissa thought.

Stella walked inside. After taking a calming deep breath, Larissa casually strolled in after her and shut the door behind her.

When the lights first came on, Larissa was too scared to open her eyes, but after she took a moment to actually look, she was quite impressed. Stella's room was really a bunch of random items all melded into one. Larissa felt it was very self-explanatory. Her walls were painted red and had band posters taped all over them. Her bed was decorated with black sheets and red pillows. Her armoire, the only thing that wasn't red or black in that room, was overflowing with clothes.

But don't think Stella would let this piece of furniture stand in her room without something gothic on it. She had stuck gothic stickers all over it.

Larissa walked up to the armoire and noticed some pictures of family and friends nicely tucked away in handcrafted frames.

"You have a cute family," Larissa said, keeping her gaze on one guy with blue eyes and curly blonde hair.

Stella was scanning through her CD collection on her rack to find some good music to play. She peeked over at Larissa. "Thanks. Dysfunctional, but cute, I guess!"

Larissa giggled. She continued to marvel over Stella's room. "Your room is so cool! It has a very gothic look to it, but the way you designed it, it's totally chic!"

Stella had just gotten done with putting her favorite CD by a band called Retro into her player. "Compared to yours, this is tacky!"

"It's so not! You have a real punk look in here, and that's really cool and different."

Stella gazed around her room. It was really nothing special, but it was definitely an upgrade from her bedroom in her old apartment in New York. "I still say it's tacky!"

"God, you really are stubborn!"

Stella giggled. "Love you too!" She pressed Play, and soon enough a guitar solo was blaring through the speakers. Stella bobbed her head to the music and began flipping through the pages of a People magazine.

The loud, droning sound of a man screaming at the top of his lungs was torture for Larissa's ears. She was more into JT and the Pussycat Dolls.

"Stella Rose, turn that God-awful song down now!" Amy yelled from below.

Stella reached over her night table and pressed Stop. "Sorry mom."

*Thank you, Mrs. Kirkpatrick*, Larissa thought. "Hey, Stella," she said.

"Yeah," she said, flipping another page.

"After today, do you wish you had stayed in New York?"

She paused. "What do you mean?"

"You know, after Cher basically messed up your day."

"Listen. I'm really trying to forget about today, okay?"

"Y––yeah, I understand. Anyway I'll pick you up tomorrow around seven, deal? That'll give me some time to make you ready to ask Chris."

Stella paused for a moment. "Nothing too crazy?"

"Promise."

"Okay."

"Great! I'll even bring my sandals along, so don't plan on wearing any shoes when I pick you up."

Stella giggled. "Sure. I'll just walk out of my house in my bedroom slippers!"

"You know what I mean!"

Stella said nothing.

Larissa smiled. "I'll see you tomorrow."

"See you then," Stella responded. "Need me to walk you to your car?"

"No, I think I can make it."

"Cool, but if I hear a loud screeching blonde outside about to be raped by some sick dude, I'll be sure to beat the crap out of him for ya!"

"Thanks." She headed towards the stairs when someone running up in the opposite direction nearly ran her over.

"Are you okay?" The person asked.

"I'm fine," she answered. She looked at the person's face. He was a tan, muscular guy with curly blonde hair and electric blue eyes. *He looks so much like Lance! This isn't him ... is he?* The guy smiled and stuck out his hand.

"I'm Jason, Stella's older brother." It was then she realized he must've been the blue-eyed-curly-haired dude from the picture.

Larissa shook his hand and stared at him for a while. *Where have you been all my life?*

"Larissa," she said. "I go to school with your sister now."

Jason smirked. "I'm glad to see you were able to handle her!"

Larissa smiled. "She's not that bad. She's actually really sweet."

"Well the one I know is sour to the core!" There was an awkward silence between them. "So were you on your way out," he asked, breaking the silence between them.

"Yeah, I was, actually."

"W—would you mind if I walked you to your car?"

"No, that would be really nice of you."

"Great, lemme just get my jacket." He raced into his bedroom and then quickly ran back out holding a blue windbreaker.

"That was fast," Larissa pointed out.

"Didn't want to keep you waiting."

Larissa tucked her blonde hair behind her ear and smiled. *You know, he's a real gentleman…just my type!* He took her hand and led her out to her car.

The car beeped as Larissa unlocked it with the remote key. Jason admired it. "That's a nice car you got there," he commented.

"Thanks. It's my dad's, actually. He let me borrow it for the day."

"My dad would never let me do that. Not after what I did to his station wagon."

"What did you do?"

He led her over to the green station wagon and pointed out a dent in the front bumper. "I accelerated into my teacher's car back in Queens when I was leaving school one day."

"No way! Did the teacher ever find out?"

"Nope! Well, he didn't know it was me."

"Slick."

"Well, I hate to brag," he joked.

Larissa giggled.

Jason admired her smile as she laughed. Her eyes gleamed under the dimmed streetlights and her teeth were as white as the snowcapped peaks of the Rocky Mountains. "You're really pretty," he blurted out. He was quickly embarrassed and lowered his head in shame.

Larissa was stunned by what he said but very flattered. "Thanks. You're pretty cool too."

*Cool?* Now, Jason felt discouraged. Did he say the wrong thing?

"Well, I better go now. See you later, Jason." She waved good-bye as she strutted down the driveway to the car. She slid into the seat and revved up the engine. Before leaving, she rolled down her window and said, "By the way, thanks for walking me to my car."

He nervously chuckled. "Don't mention it." She straightened the car up and sped away. Jason stood there watching the car fade into the night. *She is so pretty. Prettier than any girl I've ever met! I might actually like this girl . . . a lot!*

\*\*\*\*\*\*\*\*

Larissa was sprawled on her bed, wearing her pink silk pajama set. She was shopping online with her laptop on a website for a boutique based in France. She was staring at the jewelry displayed in front of her . . . but her mind was on Jason. *Oh God, he is so cute! He makes me feel special in some way I can't describe in words. The very minute I think of him, I start to feel tingly and lightheaded! I wonder if I'll see him tomorrow morning when I pick up Stella.* She thought hopefully. *I* have *to pick out a cute outfit then!* She was about to head over to her closet when her computer chimed, indicating she had an IM message. She opened the window and read the message:

**Spoiledbrat200:** Hey Larissa. Just wanted 2 c how u r. Didn't c u after school. It's like u disappeared! What happened?

It was Cher!

**Blondie01:** I thought i told you this morning. I had a spa thing 2 do with my mom 2day. We've had this planned 4 weeks now.

**Spoiledbrat200:** don't remember.   But anyways, that's so sweet! Did u have a fun time or was it just a drag?

*I had fun with my* real *friends, if that's what you mean,* Larissa thought.  That's what she wanted to type, but she decided to be the better person and tell Cher the bad news when it wasn't nearly ten o' clock on a school night!  All she really wanted was to get rid of Cher.

**Blondie01:** a little bit of both! There were times when we'd talk then there were times when she was stuck on the phone.

**Spoiledbrat200:** That sucks! Anyway I have the most AMAZING news to tell you, and it's happening tomorrow.

**Blondie01:** what?

**Spoiledbrat200:** Brittany and I are planning something completely scandalous for tomorrow's new TV morning announcement @ school. Do u want 2 know wut's ^?

**Spoiledbrat200:** hello?

**Spoiledbrat200:** Larissa, r u there?

Blondie01 has signed off @ 10:09:56 pm

Spoiledbrat200 has signed off @ 10:10:05 pm

Larissa closed her laptop. She walked over to her desk and set it down gently. She dimmed her recessed lighting before climbing into her sheets. She wasn't in the mood to hear about Cher's plan. Whatever it was, it wasn't anything good, or worth hearing! *I guess I'll just have to deal with Cher's wrath in the morning.*

Just as she was about to turn off the lights, Tootsie jumped into the bed and began licking Larissa's hand. Larissa began a fit of giggles.

"Tootsie, stop," she cried. She pulled Tootsie away from her hand and lay her down beside her. She almost immediately settled down. "Just hope mom doesn't find you here; otherwise she'll have a fit!" The dog continued panting. She leaned over and kissed Tootsie's head before resting her head on her pillow and drifting to sleep.

# *12*

Cher, Brittany, and Nadine met up in the second floor hallway to discuss the final parts of their devious plan. "What if we get in trouble?" Nadine asked.

Cher rolled her eyes. She hated it when people questioned her 'excellence.' "We won't," she replied sharply. "I've done this a hundred times before, so stop worrying!"

Nadine sighed. She was really hoping she'd get out of it, but Cher just wouldn't take no for an answer. It all started when Nadine was leaving her chauffeured Lexus and walking up to her Video Lab friends that normally sat by the front steps. Out of nowhere, the clones cornered her and ordered she'd go see Cher by the fountain A.S.A.P. At first, she was a bit intimidated. Her first thought was Cher was planning to humiliate her by throwing her into the fountain water.

"Yes, Cher," quavered Nadine as she approached Cher and her friends. "You sent for me."

"I did." She handed Brittany her nail file and continued. "Listen, cause I'm only saying it *once*. You know Stella, the new girl, right?"

She had heard of her around school, but never met her face to face. "Yeah, why?"

"She's been bothering me lately. Just recently, she snatched my best friend away from me, and I'm sure she's bent on ruling the entire school." She paced around. "I'm sure you've heard she's a drug addict, right"

"Of course, you hasn't?"

"Now, do you want someone like *that* ruling this campus?"

"N––no."

"Good. Now all I need you to do is lure her in, trap her, and I'll do the rest. Sound good?"

"Y––yes," she stammered.

Cher grinned cunningly. "That's what I want to hear. Now, this is what you're going to do, and, if you do this right, I'll reward you a hundred dollars to go towards the AP video lab." That's all Nadine had to hear before giving into Cher's commands.

Now she was standing in the middle of the second floor hall, following Cher's orders yet again. "Okay, I'll go get her." Nadine slowly entered the elevator using the student I.D. card.

Brittany spoke up. "You don't think she'll tell her, do you?"

Cher turned to Brittany. "Of course she won't, 'cause she knows the consequences, and I never break a promise."

Brittany shrugged. "If you say so."

"Oh, I *know* so!"

Nadine found Stella all by herself at her locker, applying makeup with the help of her small mirror. It looked as if she was waiting for someone. Nadine then stopped short. *I can't do this! Stella seems to be a really cool girl and she hasn't done anything to deserve this! Why can't Cher understand that? Besides that, I've never gotten in trouble, never did what I'm about to do . . . I've never even gotten a B, for Christ's sake!*

But then she remembered something else Cher had told here earlier on that day: *"I'll reward you with a hundred dollars..."*

*I can't just turn down that much money! Plus, the AP video lab needs it. . .*

"Hey," Nadine said.

Stella looked up from her mirror. "Oh, hey Nadine," she said back. She had heard about Nadine around school. "What's up?"

"Nothing much," she answered. "Just the same ol' same ol'! You?"

"I'm getting ready to ask Chris out to the Rock Fest after-party!"

"Are you for real? That's totally rad!"

"Thanks. I'm about to meet Larissa by his locker." Stella plopped the compact back into the handbag she had borrowed form Larissa. "So what do you think?"

"Marvelous——just like Grace Kelly!"

Stella grinned. "Gee, thanks. Well, gotta go. See ya!"

"Oh, don't go yet!"

She spun around again. "Did you say something," she asked.

"Yeah, I actually had to tell you some great news!"

Stella approached her. "What news?"

*Tell her! Tell her the evil plot Cher is making me do against her——but a hundred dollars can do so much for the AP lab! Oh, why does Cher have to be so rich and use her money for the wrong things!* "I just heard from a reliable source that Raul wants to ask you out to the party this weekend!"

Stella was so surprised. She had never been asked out for anything before! Well, unless you count the time in kindergarten some kid asked her to eat lunch with him by the swings. She thought back to the time she was in literature class and he had handed her Larissa's phone. His exact words to her were: "Gracias, chica." He had even said it in a low, sensual Spanish accent. *Is she sure, because I think he was just messing around? But then again, he does have some cute qualities about him. I guess I wouldn't mind going to the party with him.*

But what about Chris?

*I liked Chris long before I knew Raul even existed! Plus the girls went through all that trouble just so I'd look hot when I asked him.*

"But I was already going to ask—"

Nadine stopped her. "I know, and I'm really sorry! It's just that Raul himself asked me to tell you!"

"Seriously?"

"Totally! He even wants to meet you in private!"

"Wow!" Stella smiled. "So did he say where he wanted to meet me?"

"Yeah." She paused. *Am I really going to do this to her? She's done nothing to deserve this! But the AP video lab . . . Still, friends come before that stupid AP lab!* "Stella."

She was still staring at her with anticipation. "Yeah! What did he say?" *But I don't really know this girl! Besides, there's still no proof if that drug rumor is fake or not! And I don't want to be friends with a drug addict!* "He said to meet him right now in the second-floor hallway."

"You mean this school has more than one floor?"

"Yeah, but we barely have classes up there," she replied. "It's mostly where club meetings are held or where you go if you feel like skipping class."

"Cool. Can you lead me there?"

"Sure." Nadine led the way as the girls meandered through the clusters of teenagers all the way to the elevators. She swiped her school ID card in a slot nearby and the elevator doors whisked open. Then, in a blink of an eye, the girls entered.

Cher and Brittany were hiding behind some lockers while they waited for Nadine to come back with their prey.

"Do you think Nadine is coming back?" Brittany asked as she pinned up a loose piece of her bangs with a sparkly barrette. "It shouldn't take *this* long to drag someone up here!"

The wait was starting to annoy Cher too. She had expected everything to happen quickly, not at turtle speed! "I know," Cher began getting that evil look in her eyes—the one she got every time she was about to threaten someone. "She'd better be coming, otherwise that money I promised her is going toward my—" Suddenly, they heard the elevator doors open.

"Well, look what the cat threw up," Cher muttered.

Brittany glanced over. "Oh! So now she comes!" She let out a scoff and rolled her eyes. "This is why I do things myself!"

Nadine and Stella walked into the hallway. When they entered, Nadine noticed the two girls peeking over from the lockers. Cher winked at her as Nadine awkwardly smiled back.

Cher turned to Brittany. "Britt, get ready. The main event is about to begin..."

Nadine led her closer to the janitor's closet and sneakily checked around for any teachers and students.

It was an empty hallway.

Stella was scanning the hall, and when she didn't see Raul anywhere in sight, she asked, "So, where is he?"

Nadine swallowed hard, trying to get rid of the huge lump forming in her throat but it remained there. *I'm sorry, Stella.* She quickly opened the janitor's closet and shoved Stella in.

"Hey! Let me out!" She started banging on the door. Nadine pushed the door closed with her shoulder as she locked it with the keys she had stolen from the janitor's cart earlier that morning.

Stella continued to bang and scream for help. "Nadine, let me out now!"

Cher walked up to Nadine, giving her a standing ovation. "Good job, Nadine," she congratulated. "You have completed your task!"

"You mean this was all your fault, Cher?" Stella shouted.

"Duh! Who else would it be," she asked.

Stella let out a frustrated groan. "Cher, you'll pay for this!"

"Sure, but until then maybe you can think about how much pain you've caused me!"

"What's that supposed to mean?"

"It means stay away from Larissa! She's my friend; not yours!"

"Can't she have more than one friend?"

"Of course! Just not losers like you!"

"Fine! I'll leave Larissa alone; just let me out!" She banged the door once more. "At least let me out so I can ask Chris to the party this weekend!"

"Hmm… I've decided to ask Chris to the party! I'm sure he'll have more fun with someone with a little more class, if you know what I mean?"

"Cher, you can't—"

"I can, and I will!" She turned to the girls behind her. "Let's go." Cher led the way as Brittany and Nadine followed.

"So you're just going to leave me here?" Stella screamed.

"Looks that way!" Brittany snapped and walked into the elevator with Cher and Nadine. The girls rode it down to the first floor.

Once they were gone, Stella began banging the door and screaming for help again. "Someone, help me! I'm trapped!" She paused for a moment to catch her breath. "Anybody?"

But there was no one in the hallway to hear her plea.

********

Cher, Brittany, and Nadine reached the first-floor hallway and moved on to stage two of their plan. They met at Cher's locker to go over it once more.

"Does anyone know where Raul is," Cher asked.

"He's usually at the girls' bathroom, hitting on the girls that come around," Nadine answered.

Brittany rolled her eyes. "He's such a freak," she exclaimed. "What does Stella see in him anyway?"

"She's probably desperate, or she wouldn't have believed Nadine!" Brittany and Cher let out some giggles while thinking about Stella struggling to escape.

Nadine, on the other hand, was still feeling guilty about what she had done to Stella. She really liked Stella as a friend and thought she was really a sweet person. *And I highly doubt Stella's a drug addict! Cher probably made that up just to embarrass her.*

"Let's find go him!" Nadine heard Cher say. Brittany followed Cher toward the bathrooms. Nadine quickly ran up to them.

Sure enough, Raul and his best friend, Mike, were standing by the girls' bathroom, chatting with a tenth grader who appeared to be bored with him.

Cher stopped short and turned to Nadine. "You still have the keys, right?" she asked. Nadine had her hands in her dress pocket and jingled the keys to indicate she had them. Cher smiled. "Good." She then turned to Brittany. "Are you ready?"

"I was born ready!" Brittany spruced up her hair, smoothed out her black and white Diane von Furstenburg bubble dress, swiped on some lip gloss and finally walked over to Raul. "Wish me luck," she called out.

"My fingers are crossed!" Cher shouted back at her.

"Hey, Raul," Brittany said when she reached him.

He stared at her. "Hey," he replied. "What can I do for you this fine day, pretty lady?" Brittany nearly let out a burst of laughter after hearing that corny pickup line.

"Don't flatter yourself," muttered Brittany under her breath.

"What did you say?"

"Never mind. Anyway can you do me this one itty-bitty favor?"

"Sure. Name your price."

"Can you walk me up to the second-floor hallway?" She batted her eyelashes. "I'm almost late for my mock trial meeting."

"But why do you need me to walk you up there," he asked.

Brittany leaned closer to his body. *Yuck! He reeks of cheap cologne and … I think it's a skunk.* She tried her best to hold her breath. "I'll get scared." She tapped her finger on his chest. "You don't want me all alone up there, do you," she whined, pouting her already-perfectly-pouted lips.

Raul grinned. He just couldn't say no to a girl that was practically breathing down his neck! *Dang! She's so lucky she's hot!* "All right." He finally gave in.

*Yes!* Brittany cheered in her mind.

He held out his arm, but Brittany smiled politely and rejected his offer.

"It's okay. I can walk on my own," she answered modestly.

"That's cool." They walked side by side until they reached Cher and Nadine around the corner. Raul went ahead as Brittany lingered behind. Nadine slipped the keys into her clutch before she caught up with Raul.

Stella was sitting on what she thought was a bucket full of grout, hoping she wouldn't die young in, of all places, a janitor's closet. *There has to be someone coming to look for me*, she thought hopefully, but the way things looked, it wouldn't be happening anytime soon! *I guess I'll never marry Jason Dolley, go to France for a year, or be able to finally be a size B cup!*

Suddenly, she heard some footsteps walking down the hall. *Yes! My worries are now over! I will go to France, I will be a B cup (eventually), and I will marry JD!* She began banging on the door and screaming again.

"Help! Help me, somebody! I'm trapped in the closet!"

Raul heard the noises. "What was that?" He asked Brittany.

Brittany knew it was Stella. "Who cares?" But Raul wasn't buying her story, so he walked toward the sound.

"It sounds like someone's locked in there."

Brittany quickly ran up to him. "Then why don't you find out what it is?" She quickly opened the door and propelled him into the closet. She propped her body against the door as Raul tried to fight back until finally she locked it.

"Brittany, let me out," he shouted, yanking the doorknob.

"I'm sorry, did you say something?"

"Brittany, you lied to me!"

She shrugged. "Wouldn't be the first time I lied to a boy as stupid as you!"

"But I thought you liked me!" he said to her. "I mean, you flirted and everything!"

She let out a scoff. "Get real," she snapped. "Why would I like some deadbeat like you?" She placed the keys in her purse. "Anyway, you lovebirds have fun in there! I'll be back to check on you later." She walked back over to the elevator and rode it down to the first floor.

Cher and Nadine were waiting by Cher's locker. When Cher spotted Brittany walking toward them with a happy expression on her face, Cher grew happier as well. She had a good feeling the job had been done.

"What happened?" Cher asked when Brittany reached the girls. "Tell all the details!"

"Perfect! He's now trapped in the closet with Stella . . . and it sounds like they'll be having plenty of fun up there!" She looked over at Nadine, who was staring down at the parquet floor. "Here you go, Nadine."

Nadine looked up from her dirty Reeboks. Brittany handed her the janitor's keys. She snatched them from her and put them back in her pocket.

"Excellent," Cher commented. "Now we're on to stages three and four."

"You mean there's *more*," asked Nadine.

"Duh! We can't just lock them in there and be done with it. Cher just doesn't work that way."

Cher turned to Nadine. "Think you can handle it?" she asked.

"Sure. I've come this far, haven't I?"

Cher rolled her eyes. "Whatever! Anyway, all I need you to do is go to Carter's office, hand her the keys, and tell her you found the keys in Stella's locker and you suspect she's up there with someone."

"Are you sure?"

"Don't question me! Just do it!" Cher shot her an evil glare. Nadine tried not to be intimidated by Cher's death look, but it was really starting to scare her.

"Okay. I'll meet you guys after my afternoon announcement."

"Which reminds me—do you think you'd be able to add Stella's 'rendezvous' to your little show?"

*Why don't you do this dirty work yourself?*

"And you know, if you say yes, I'll add fifty dollars to that 'paycheck' of yours, but if you say no, those one hundred fifty dollars is going back into my wallet. Understood?"

*Ooh, she's evil!* "Fine," Nadine murmured.

"Great," she looked down at her watch. "Well, I have some––business to attend to. See you on TV!" She quickly left the scene and headed over to her secret third stage of the operation: get Chris to be her date.

*******

"What do you mean she stole the keys to the janitor's closet," Principal Carter bellowed.

"It's true, Principal Carter. I went to her locker, as usual, to put her books away whiles she went to the nurse to take her medication. But this time, I found those keys in there." she pointed at the large ring of keys sitting on Carter's desk. "I suspect she must've had one of her friends lock her up there with a guy."

Principal Carter tapped her pencil against her cherry desk furiously. She was busily trying to think of the best punishment for this. Finally, she shot up from her desk chair. "Yamaguchi," she called out.

The vice principal sauntered into the room. "Yes, Principal Carter."

"Go up to the second-floor janitor's closet and bring me back those two hooligans who have locked themselves in there and are now possibly engaging in suggestive activities."

"Yes, ma'am."

Yamaguchi was about to leave the office when Carter called back out to her. "You may want these." Yamaguchi turned around and noticed Carter holding up a ring of keys. She took the keys from her and left the office.

Once she was gone, Carter congratulated Nadine on her 'good' work. "Thank you, Ms. Potter. You may return to your classes."

Nadine smiled and left the office. She took a deep breath after she left the room and closed the door behind her. *I am so going to hell for this!*

**Cher and Brittany's plan: not. cool.**

**Stella's fate after Yamaguchi finds her with Raul: well . . . you can probably just guess for that one!**

Cher stood only three feet away from her newest crush—so close, she could almost smell his neck. He was standing next to his locker, talking on his cell phone. She really wished Brittany was there to assure her she was pretty and there was no way Chris could turn her down. But she was alone. *Keep it cool, Cher. You've dealt with his kind in the past, so this should be a piece of cake.*

"Hey," she said in a seductive voice when she approached him.

"Yo, Tre, lemme call you back...yea...iight, peace." He hung up and put his full attention on Cher. "So, what's up with you, Cher?"

"Nothing, just thinking about stuff."

"Stuff like what," he grinned.

She rolled her shoulders back to give the impression her boobs were much larger. "Well, I've been thinking there's a huge party going on this Saturday, and I have no one to go with?"

"Funny. Neither do I?"

"So does that mean you're available?"

"I—" His phone buzzed again. He stared down at his caller I.D. "I gotta take this call. Can we talk later?"

"But—" He had already left before Cher had a chance to speak. Standing in that desolate hallway and literally being walked out on by the cutest guy she had ever seen, she really hated herself for putting all that effort into looking like Naomi Campbell that morning.

# 13

"Where's Stella?" Larissa asked as she set down her plate of chicken salad with no dressing. "I was supposed to help her ask Chris out today for the Rock Fest after-party, but she never showed."

Tara came up and sat down next to her.

"I don't know where she is," she admitted. "In fact, I haven't seen her since this morning."

"Do you think she's avoiding us?" Jade asked after taking a sip of her Pepsi.

Gia took a bite out of her sandwich and swallowed it before she spoke. "I wouldn't think so." Just then, all the mounted televisions in the cafeteria turned on and Nadine appeared on the screen.

"Why's Nadine on TV," Jade asked.

"Her news show is starting today!" Tara announced.

"Oh yeah! I remember the announcement from last year." Jade commented.

Nadine fixed her posture in her seat and began delivering the news. "Good afternoon, students, and this is my new show. During this half-hour show, I'll give you the inside scoop on our school! They may even involve your own best friend!"

Almost all the girls and boys in the cafeteria let out gasps and started passing glances over to their friends. Larissa, Gia, Jade, and Tara didn't do that. They knew they could trust each other.

"And as my first report," she said, tucking her hair behind her ear, "Hiroshi Sushi in the cafeteria will be shut down for two weeks due to food poisoning." Everyone made 'ew' sounds, and some even projected fake vomiting noises.

"Our next report has to do with the student body. Vice-principal Yamaguchi has just caught new girl Stella Kirkpatrick and Raul Sanchez in the second-floor janitor's closet in the middle of getting their freak on!"

At this point, everyone started laughing his or her head off.

"I always knew that girl was a whore," one girl cried out. She was sitting two tables down from Larissa and her friends.

Her friend sitting next to her nodded in agreement, "me to. Did you see what she was wearing this morning? It was so revealing! *I* don't even wear clothes like that!"

Larissa exchanged glances with her friends. They all seemed as shocked as she was. "Stella? Locked in the janitor's closet with Raul," she shouted.

"That is so gross!" Jade exclaimed. She even dropped her chicken sandwich on the ground. "What was she thinking?"

"Nothing, obviously!" Gia said.

Larissa wasn't convinced Stella would do such a thing. *That doesn't sound like her at all!* "Guys, we can't prove that Stella actually intended to do that!"

"We have proof!" Tara pointed at the screen. "Nadine just announced it on the TV!"

"Yeah, but I'm still not so sure." Larissa then scoured the room for her main suspect—Cherisse Ann von Seaton.

She found her sitting with Brittany, Carlos, T. J., Mitchell, Tommy, and Jenny at Café Renee, laughing their heads off. But when everyone was caught in the moment of laughing, Brittany and Cher gave each other high-fives. At that point, Larissa was convinced that Cher and Brittany had done this!

"It wasn't Stella!" Larissa called out to her friends. They looked at her as if she were crazy.

"What are you talking about?" Gia asked.

"It was Cher and Brittany! I know it!" The three girls thought for a moment. It made perfect sense! Cher hated

Stella for some dumb reason, and now she was out to seek her downfall!

"Okay, maybe you're right," Tara confessed.

"Then what do we do about this?" Jade asked.

"We first have to find some way to clear Stella's name." Larissa stole another glance at Cher. "Then we get even!"

"How?" Gia asked once more.

"I'll tell you guys later, but first we have to save our friend from possible suspension."

"Right!" Tara shouted. The girls then threw out their paper plates and rushed over to Principal Carter's office.

*******

"Thanks for saving me," Stella said once the girls had left Principal Carter's office in one piece.

"No problem," Larissa answered. "That's what friends do."

The girls were able to plead enough on Stella's behalf to let her off with just a warning.

"It wasn't her fault," Tara said to Principal Carter. "She could've been locked in there by someone else."

"But who?" Everyone wanted to say it was Cher but couldn't find the heart to rat on her. It would only mean trouble for them. Carter turned to Stella. "Well, who was it?"

"I—I'm not sure," Stella stammered. "It happened so fast, I wasn't able to see the face." *The last thing I need is for Cher to hunt me down and literally kill me!*

Carter let out a sigh. "Well, I guess since you are telling me you didn't lock yourself up there, I can't suspend you."

The girls cheered in triumph.

"But I can let you off with a warning." She waved her finger, complete with a manicured red nail, in Stella's face. "The next time I hear something about you conducting childish behavior, you will be asked to leave the school forever!"

Stella gulped.

"Understood?"

"Yes, ma'am."

"Good. Now you may leave."

The girls went on their way to their afternoon classes.

"What really happened?" Jade inquired.

Stella sighed heavily. "Nadine locked me in the janitor's closet because Cher bribed her with money."

"Are you serious," exclaimed Gia.

"Yeah," Stella answered sadly.

"She should so be suspended," explained Jade. "It's in the rulebook that bribery on school campus in unacceptable!"

"It's too late now!" Larissa shouted. "You should've thought of that *before* we left Carter's office."

"Now how will we get back at her," Tara asked.

Stella quickly shook her head. "Is it too late to ask Chris to the party?"

Larissa shook her head. "No. I haven't heard he's taken yet."

"Good. Think you can help me find him?" The two girls smiled at each other. They had a feeling of where it was going.

"Duh! Let's go!" The two girls hurried down the hall toward his locker.

"You go get him, girl!" Tara shouted out to them.

"We're rooting for you!" Jade added.

"Try not to snort like a pig if he tells a funny joke!" Gia yelled.

"Okay!" Stella called out. The girls continued jogging down the hall, trying their best not to fall in their heels.

Stella and Larissa had finally reached Chris's locker. Now he was talking with some friends of his. Because they hated the food selection in the cafeteria, him and his boys snuck out to eat cheese steaks from a deli only a block from school. The girls stopped short before Stella

Larissa turned to Stella to give her last-minute encouragement. "This is it," she squealed. "Are you nervous?"

"Of course! I mean it's him!"

"Don't worry. You'll be fine, just remember to relax and the rest will follow through!"

"Easy for you to say! I bet you have guys drooling all over you!"

Larissa paused for a moment. *I wish!* She didn't want to admit she never had been asked out. Besides, right now was about Stella.

"This isn't about me. It's about you asking Chris to the Rock Fest after-party before Cher does. Okay?"

Stella took a calming deep breath. "Right," she smiled and ambled over to the group of guys. Larissa hid around the corner to observe.

"Hi," Stella said.

"Aren't you the girl who was locked in the closet with that faggot," Chris's friend, Will asked.

"Yo, Will, you know what I just thought," Chris's other friend, Vincent said.

"What?"

"She just came *out* of the closet!" He laughed at the joke, but he was the only one who did.

Stella stood there staring at her painted toenails.

"Cool it, Vince."

"Sorry, man," he wiped a tear from his eye. "Well, I'll leave you two alone." He bid farewell to Chris and walked away. Will tagged along.

"So you're the girl everyone's talking about," Chris said to her when his friends left.

Stella forced a smile. "Yeah, that's me. I'm the girl who was found locked in the janitor's with Raul . . . but just for the record, I don't like him!"

Chris chuckled. "I figured you didn't. He didn't seem to be your type."

Stella smiled. *At least he wasn't laughing at me.*

"Anyway, what can I do for you, Stella?"

She twirled a red ringlet of her hair around her finger. *Why didn't I rehearse this with Larissa in the car? Oh man! Well . . . here goes nothing!* "I was wondering . . . are you going to the rock test . . . no, I mean the rock pest . . . no! What I'm trying to say is . . ."

"Are you trying to ask me out to the Rock *Fest* party," Chris asked, making it a point to emphasize the "Fest".

Stella let out a sigh of relief. "Yeah." They were quiet for a moment. She wasn't sure if he was going to say a slow yes or a slow no.

"Sure. I'd love to go with you."

"Really," she shouted louder than she wanted. She ducked her head away for a moment to prevent him from seeing her cheeks redden. She gazed up again. He was still staring at her with those beautiful brown eyes.

"Really." He grazed her chin gently with his finger. "You know, you lucked out. Cher come around earlier to ask me."

"Are you serious?" *This means he chose* me *over* her! The thought alone made Stella feel giddy all over. She couldn't wait to tell her friends––and see the expression on Cher's face.

"So should I pick you up Saturday around seven?" Chris's deep voice startled Stella.

"Uh, yea, but can we meet here instead." The last thing she needed was Chris meeting her embarrassing parents, who would take pictures for twenty minutes, and her super-annoying brother belching in his face!

Nope! It was better to meet at the school.

"Sure. See you later." He winked at her before he grabbed his life science book out of the open locker behind him and walked down the hall.

Once she was sure he was far away, Stella started jumping up and down and ran up to where she left Larissa. She jumped out as soon as she saw Stella run up.

"What happened? What did he say? Give me details!"

"There's not much to explain . . . except I have a date this Saturday!"

Larissa screamed almost as loud as Stella did. "I can't believe it," she said.

"I know, and guess what?"

"What?"

"He told me Cher asked him earlier and he chose me over her!"

"No way!"

"Believe it," she paused, "and I owe it all to you!"

"What did I do?"

"You gave me confidence, Larissa. Without you, there's no way I could've asked Chris, or even face Cher with my head held high."

It was at this moment Larissa was sure Stella was the answer. Not only did she succeed in abandoning Cher, but she also made a best friend in the process. "I'm glad I was here to help." They hugged each other dearly.

"You're my BFF too," Stella divulged. And it didn't matter if everyone was leaving the cafeteria now and staring at them strangely. All they cared about was each other.

**Cher and no date (Ha ha ha ha ha!): 0 points.**

**Stella and her hot date with Chris (Yay!): 5 points.**

# 14

It was five in the evening, and Cher and Brittany were sipping piña coladas by Cher's massive six-foot-deep in-ground pool. They had just come back from a long afternoon shopping spree in Las Vegas——Cher had flown out on her private jet. She needed a place far enough away to clear her mind from school. So after spending over six thousand dollars on her father's credit card and now chilling by the pool, she felt she was pretty stable.

But it's still wasn't fair.

If not her, who else would Chris take to the party? Certainly not Brittany. She knew for a fact she wasn't his type——she was too clingy! Not Jenny, or Larissa. Who could it be?

"So how many times a week does he go to their house?" Brittany asked as she swirled her straw around in her glass.

Cher looked up at her next-door neighbor's pool man skim for debris. He had nice arm muscle, but there was really nothing special about him to her. He was just another one of the guys. Chris was the only man that stuck out in her mind.

"Mondays and Fridays," she said unflappably.

Brittany sipped her drink. "I am so coming over!"

*You wish you could! I'm not putting up with you But two days after school too!" if you're that desperate, why don't you go back to butt ugly ex-boyfriend of yours—Brent!* "Whatever."

"So, have you been up-to-date with the latest gossip around school?"

"Hello, we're not in school!"

She grabbed her phone and held it up. "It's called text messaging!"

Cher rolled her eyes. "Whatever! Just tell me what's up?"

Brittany pulled down her oversized sunglasses and leaned back in her chair. "Well, word on the street is Chris Tyler——"

"What about Chris?" She shot up from her chair.

"Calm down, chica. It's not a big deal——well, okay maybe it——"

"Just tell me what's going on," Cher spat.

"Chris Tyler is going to the Rock Fest after-party with Stella Kirkpatrick."

No amount of sadness could've overcome how Cher felt right then. *So she's the one he's going with?* For the longest time, Cher couldn't speak. How could she allow this to happen to her? What would the people at school think of her?

"Who cares," she mumbled, trying to sound like she could care less. She adjusted her brown Juicy Couture bikini top that felt like it was slipping off. "Then why do I feel so betrayed?"

"I knew it," Brittany peered over her shades.

Cher glared at her peculiarly. "Knew what?"

"You totally have a crush on Chris!"

She sighed. There was no reason to hide her feelings now. Brittany had found out. "Well, yes, I do. Happy?"

"Of course I'm happy for my friend!" Brittany sucked on a piece of ice. "You two would make a cute couple like Will and Jada Pinkett-Smith."

"But it's so unfair! I mean, if I'm the most desirable girl at school––no offense, Britt––why doesn't he like me?" She shot up from her seat and began pacing back and forth on the hot patio. "I deserve to be Chris's date tomorrow, and not that wretched fool!

Brittany watched as her friend marched in front of her. "No question!"

"I look better than she'll ever look!"

"Obviously!"

"Plus, who does she think she is, stealing away my crush! The high school code says no male or female should steal another student's significant or soon-to-be significant other!"

"Where does it say that," Brittany asked dumbfounded.

Cher rolled her eyes. "Nowhere, it's just there!"

"Oh!"

"God! You are so clueless sometimes!"

"Sorry!"

"Whatever! You're forgiven!"

Brittany smiled. "Thanks."

Cher went deep into thought. *I have to do something about this . . . or else Stella will win Chris's heart, and I'll be left high and dry! This could even cost my dignity.* She turned to Brittany, who was lying still in her seat, soaking up the rays.

"Brittany, what would you do if you liked a guy but he probably liked someone else," she asked.

Brittany propped up on her elbows. "Well, I think she should feel the same pain–maybe even more––than you feel."

"So what's your idea?" Cher asked, hoping the answer to all her current problems would be solved.

"Don't worry about that," Brittany responded coolly. "Just know that I'll have the best plan ever by tomorrow night."

"If you say so, but if it sucks, I'm holding you personally responsible!"

Brittany glared icily at her. *What is she trying to say? That's she's the only girl in the world who can think up an ingenious plan?*

"Well, guess again, Cher. This plan will be flawless. Trust me!" *That should show her I'm not afraid of her warnings!*

"Whatever." Cher murmured quietly and went back to relaxing in her lounge chair. "It's your neck on the line; not mine."

Brittany said nothing and just lay back on her chair, wondering if maybe helping Cher wasn't such a great idea?

# 15

Stella was rushing to straighten her hair in front of the fogged-up mirror in the upstairs bathroom. Her brother had taken a thirty-minute-long shower after his soccer practice. "Ouch," she yelped. She had accidentally burned her thumb with the flat iron. *I hope Chris hasn't been waiting too long*, she thought.

That would be her worst nightmare.

She finished the last bundle of hair before turning the iron off and setting it back down on the sink counter. She then pulled out the ruby red lipstick she borrowed from her mother and applied it on her lips. When she was done, she smacked her lips together and went on to the next task: putting on her black combat boots, which would tie her rocker look together, which consisted of an eighties ruffled miniskirt——again something she "borrowed" from her mother's closet——a leather jacket over a plain white tank, and finally ripped tights.

The boots were buried underneath a pile of clothes that were supposed to be in the laundry hamper and old magazine issues. She slipped them on and lastly, before stepping out of her room, gazed at her reflection one last time in the mirror. She wasn't drop-dead gorgeous, but she was pretty decent. All of a sudden, she felt so un-confident. *Does Chris like hot girls? What if Chris is only "playing" me just to get a laugh out of it?* The thought alone was enough to make her hurl.

"Hey, Chris," she thought of herself standing in the school parking lot in front of Chris's motorcycle. The sky was lit up with stars and the light breeze wisped through her soft hair.

"Stella? You actually came?" He didn't seem so happy.

"Yeah," she said slowly. "Why, you had your doubts?"

"No, it's just that––" Soon, a Bentley came rolling up towards the two, and a gorgeous five foot five African American female strutted looking radiant in a designer dress and pumps. She looked just like a model.

But the girl she saw wasn't any model.

It was Cher.

"Oh, it's you, loser," Cher signaled to her driver to leave before strolling up to Chris's side and kissed his cheek. "What do you want with my man?"

As much as Stella wanted to say something, the words just weren't coming out. Her brain had been temporarily put on halt.

"Well, say something?" Cher was growing impatient.

"I––is this your girlfriend, Chris?"

"Uh, yea. I thought I told you this?"

"What! You didn't tell me anything? You asked *me* out remember?"

He turned to Cher, "can you believe this girl? She actually thought I asked her out!" He began laughing and soon after, Cher joined in too.

Stella stood there in deep shock. She wanted to cry and let Chris know he was nothing but a jerk and Cher was just plain evil, but she had to be strong. Breaking down now was just too risky. "Can someone please tell me what's going on?"

Cher let out a groan and said, "Look, new girl. Chris would never go out with the likes of you. He only asked you because we got into a fight earlier on. Now"––she placed her hand on his chiseled chest––"we're back together, and you are out of luck! See ya!" And that's the part of the nightmare Cher straddled on the back of Chris's Suzuki, and the two drove off, leaving Stella in the dust.

A knock on the door woke her back up. "Stella, can I come in?"

"Jason, go away! It's bad enough you made me late!"

"Aw, c'mon! Just for a sec, please?" He managed to peek his head into her room.

"Alright, but make it quick!"

Jason smiled and slammed the door behind him. "I need your help."

"With?" Stella crossed her arms across her chest.

"Do you remember that girl you came here with the other night?"

"You mean Larissa?"

"Yeah, Larissa."

"What about her?"

"Is she . . . is she seeing anyone?"

"How am I supposed to know," she asked "I just met her two days ago!"

"I know you know the truth! You guys hang out almost every day after school!"

Stella grunted. She hated it when her brother was right. "Fine! She's not."

"Has she told you she likes anyone?"

Stella groaned again. "Why are you asking me all these questions?" Jason opened his mouth, but she didn't bother to hear his answer. "Look, I'm late for my party as it is!" She stormed past him and was close to reaching the steps when her brother blocked her way and knelt down on his knees.

"Please, Stella. We're siblings! We have to help each other out!"

"And have you ever helped me out in any way?" He stopped to think. "Exactly, you haven't!"

"Okay, you're right, but please, sis, help me!"

Stella glowered down at his face just to be sure he wasn't delaying time intentionally. But when she saw his eyes, they were wide like a puppy dog begging to be pet. *Maybe he isn't lying. He really* does *my need help!*

"Okay, maybe I can help you—"

Jason shot up and hugged his sister. "Sis, you rule!"

Stella quickly peeled him off her. "I said I'd help you; not become your best friend!"

"Sorry. So, does she like anyone?"

"I doubt it.  If she does, she's never told me." Stella stared up at the grandfather clock in the corner.  It was a quarter past eight. *Chris has to be wondering where I am by now?* "But if you're that serious, hurry up and change. Then you can drive me to my school to meet Chris and follow us to the party. I'm pretty sure she'll be there."

"Sweet! I'll be done in a flash!" He rushed into his bedroom to change.

Jason came out immediately afterwards, wearing a short-sleeved navy blue T-shirt, shorts, and flip-flops.

"That was quick," Stella stated.

"Told you I was serious."

"Well, in that case, let's go." They walked down the stairs toward the living room.

They found their mother in the living room, reading a book. "Hi, Mom! Bye, Mom!" Stella quickly shouted out.

Amy glanced up from her book. "Jason, you're going with her?"

"Actually, I've decided to drop her off at her school to meet her date; maybe even head over to the party for a few hours."

Amy smiled. "That's nice. I love to see you guys bonding!"

Jason and Stella forced a giggle.

*Please, Mom! We are so not bonding!* Stella thought. "Yeah. Anyway, we're leaving," she said.

"Okay. Be back by eleven."

"We will." Stella rushed over to the door before her mom could talk any more. She was known for talking for lengthy amounts of time. Jason grabbed his car keys off the hook and followed Stella outside.

\*\*\*\*\*\*\*\*

Stella and Chris arrived at the hotel fifteen minutes late (Jason ditched them to go over to the pool once they reached the party). "You look great," Chris whispered into her ear right before they entered the hotel's pool terrace.

Her cheeks reddened. "Thanks. You're looking handsome too." He wore some board shorts with flip-flops and a black muscle shirt––pretty hot if you ask me. With Chris on her arm, she was oozing with confidence. No one could judge her because she'd simply tell them, "you wish you had him!" It may have sounded a bit to Cher-like, but she was feeling so wonderful at the moment, who cared if she acted like Cher! She would be the life of the party, and that's all that mattered.

As they made their way to the bar, a lot of the partygoers began to gossip.

"Since when do they go out," she heard one girl wearing a printed Shoshanna strapless one - piece with a pair of Valentino thong sandals with a low heel ask her friend sitting next to her poolside.

Her friend took a sip of her margarita and glared up at the pair as they strode on by. "I heard he's using her to make some other chick jealous," she answered.

Another girl who was standing near the refreshments wearing nothing but a Stella McCartney bikini and black Juicy sarong noticed the couple walking towards them, stopping to chat with some people along the way. She leaned closer to whisper to her friend nearby. "I heard she was having sex with Raul in the closet before she was found!"

"I heard from Haylie that she admitted she liked Raul in a text message between her and Cher," the girl's friend responded.

These were only some of the things she heard people say.

Stella was a little disturbed by their comments, but she knew gossip was always lies anyway. *I don't like Raul and I regret being locked in that smelly closet with him! And I hope Chris isn't using me!*

"Why is everyone staring at us," she asked Chris.

"Ignore 'em. There nothing but hussies anyway!"

Stella beamed with joy after he said that. Maybe Chris wasn't the guy she thought he was—he did have scruples after all.

And that's exactly her kind of man.

*******

Cher gulped down her Coke mixed with rum. She didn't care if she would get so drunk, she wouldn't be able to get home, and her father would scream at her for drinking illegally again. All she wanted to feel was the sting and the pain that came with the drink. The same pain and sting she felt now.

"You really need to calm down," Brittany told her after she set down her strawberry smoothie. She chose not to indulge herself into alcohol that night. "I told you I have everything under control.

221

"But still it's not fair," Cher threw her empty Coke can at the back wall of the bar. She nearly broke down in tears. "He should be with me!"

The bartender came up, banging the can on top of the counter. "Hey, lady, if you wanted more, all you had to do was ask."

Cher drunkenly stared up at him and was just about ready to smack his prickly cheek when she heard, "hey, guys," come from behind. She turned her head, and what she saw made all the color from her face go.

It was Stella and Chris.

"Hey," Brittany replied flatly.

Cher was too stunned to speak. *This is just the beginning. Next, they'll be feeding each other and before I know it, they'll be married and have ugly babies!*

"So what are you guys doing just sitting around?" Chris asked. "Shouldn't you be mingling with your other friends?"

Cher's gaze went from Stella to Chris. *What's wrong with sitting down for a change?* Cher thought. *And besides, it's none of his business whether we feel like hanging out with our friends or not!* "We're waiting for a better song to come on," she answered calmly. "This wannabe rock band, Charm, or whatever you call it, is getting on my last nerve!"

The band was performing their smash hit, <u>Don't Treat Me Like A Toy</u>, up on stage. Some of the students in attendance were bobbing their heads to the music. She took another sip of her drink to keep the conversation minimal. She couldn't possibly be seen speaking with the traitor who came with Stella, now being called slut by some.

"Oh," Chris replied. He wasn't used to Cher being so quiet around him. Most of the time, she would be all over him, laughing at everything he said and junk. *Is she mad at something or me?*

"Yeah, anyway, we'll meet you on the dance floor," Brittany said.

"Cool," he smiled. He then looked over at Cher, who was trying to hide her face from Chris. "I'll save you a dance, Cher?" he offered.

Stella awkwardly fixed her skirt. He hadn't asked *her* to dance yet, his *date*!

Being the girl she was, Cher stuck to her selfish pride. "I'll be okay." *"You can go dance with your little friend now,"* she wanted to add, but she decided to smile instead.

"If you say so," he turned to Stella. "Ready to dance?"

Stella first stole a glimpse of Cher, who didn't show she was envious of the attention, but knew she was, and told him, "yes. I'd love to dance." When his back was turned, she stuck her tongue out at Cher and before she knew it, she was jumping up and down with Chris right behind her.

As soon as the couple left, Cher quickly spun Brittany around in her barstool to confront her. "You'd better have a plan ready," she threatened.

Brittany brushed Cher's hand off her tan shoulder. "Chill! I have a plan!"

Cher's eyes beamed with joy. "Really," she exclaimed. "What is it?"

Brittany took another sip of her smoothie before she answered, "Sorry, can't tell you just yet."

Cher's happy expression dropped. "Why?"

"Because it's a surprise, duh!" Brittany set her drink down on the bar and stood up. But before she walked over to the DJ table, she turned back around to Cher. "But meet me at the DJ booth in, like, ten minutes!"

"Ten minutes," Cher snapped. "I can't wait that long!"

"Well, this time, you have to. Toodles!" She walked over to the plump African American male to discuss her plan (without all the vivid details) with him.

********

Larissa, Jade, Gia, and Tara came in around nine thirty. The party was in full swing by then. Almost everybody was dancing on the concrete around the pool to the hip-hop soundtrack that was playing.

"This party is sick," Gia shouted as she tried to jam to the music, but rather than looking like the coolest dancer in the room, she looked more like a lady with back problems.

"I hope we didn't miss Charm," Jade said.

Tara glanced over at the makeshift stage. She couldn't spot any band equipment or people. Well, there were a few drunks dancing up there, but none of them were a part of the band Charm. "I think we did," she responded.

"Man! I really was looking forward to seeing them perform."

"It's cool!" Gia assured her. "We can dance instead." The girls looked at her confusingly. Gia was the last person they thought would actually suggest dancing. She had two left feet!

"Are you feeling okay," Larissa asked, feeling her forehead for her temperature.

Gia gently took Larissa's hand off her forehead. "I'm perfectly fine," she shouted. "I just want to do something fun for a change."

Tara smiled. "I'm down with that! Let's go dance!" The two girls hurried over to the dance floor.

Jade turned to Larissa. "Is it okay if I go dance with them too," she asked sheepishly.

Larissa grinned. *I love it when she's this polite.* "Sure," Larissa said to her. "Go have a ball!"

"Thanks." Jade joined her friends on the dance floor and began dancing with them. They looked like a bunch of idiots jumping around, but as long as they were having fun, they were fine with looking like complete dorks! And that's what Larissa loved about them.

If she had come with Cher, they wouldn't be on the dance floor; they'd be either gossiping about people or mingling around the bar with other popular people! Basically, going to a party with Cher was a drag. She never did anything fun like talk with guys (Cher always had to have the cutest boy there) nor could she go off to meet other people (Cher feared she'd look stupid). *At least now I can be free from that controlled environment and be happy with normal teenage girls like me!*

A senior with shaggy brown hair and bright, green eyes walked past her. "How's it goin', cutie," he asked her.

Larissa began to say something, but a person from behind grabbed her by the shoulder, causing her to yelp. "There you are," said the person.

The guy chuckled, saying, "kids," and went to go flirt with senior girls lounging on the chaises.

"Stella," Larissa wailed.

"What?"

"You just ruined my chances with that guy!"

"Oh, forget about him." She pulled her towards the refreshment table. "I have more problems at hand."

"What's going on?"

Stella stopped short and pointed her eyes in the direction of Chris, who was grinding with some girls who clearly dressed like hookers. Larissa glanced in the same direction. "Hey, isn't that Chris?"

"That's the problem. He won't ask me to dance, but he'd rather dance with those...sluts! I mean, we only danced once to some stupid Charm song!"

Larissa put her hands on Stella's bare shoulders. She had taken off her jacket and left it at the front desk with the receptionist. "Breathe, Stella."

Stella did as she was told.

"It's fine. According to the magazines, it's better to give your date some room. This will let him know that you aren't possessive or clingy."

She let out a sigh. "I guess. Thanks for the advice, Ms. Advice Columnist."

Larissa let out a hearty laugh. "What can I say, I was made to help the people!"

The girls made their way through the crowd towards the table.

There weren't much people there, just the losers who couldn't dance and chose to watch the popular kids have the time of their lives.

"How do you think they move like that," one Chinese nerd asked his friend.

"Well, I have hypothesized that somewhere in their DNA is a gene allowing them to move with such rhythm." His friend clapped at his own achievement in science.

"What dorks," Larissa muttered.

Stella giggled into her palms and reached out for a turkey and ham sandwich. "Oh, before I forget, I have a person here I'd like for you to meet."

"Really? Who," Larissa muffled. She had already dug into the slice of vanilla cake.

Stella tapped on the shoulder of a guy who was gazing out the window onto Los Angeles' skyline. "She's here," she whispered.

Jason turned around, and when his eyes met with Larissa's sea-blue ones, his insides melted. She was like a fantasy he had always wanted.

"Larissa, I'd like for you to meet my brother, Jason. Jas, this is my West Coast best friend, Larissa."

"You again," Larissa whispered. A slow smile crept across her bronzed face, letting Jason know it was okay to talk to her.

"It's so nice to see you," he hushed back.

"Is there a reason why you guys are whispering," Stella asked the two.

Both Larissa and Jason landed back on earth and shook their hands like normal 'unacquainted' people would. "I'm Jason."

"Larissa."

They stared at each other for the longest time, forgetting they were still holding hands.

"Okay, this is *beyond* weird," Stella spat. "Do you guys know each other already or something?"

Larissa shook his head. "No, he just looks vaguely familiar, that's all." She winked at him when Stella wasn't paying attention.

Jason grinned back.

"Uh huh," Stella still wasn't convinced.

It was then Jason decided it was time he left before there was tension. "Well, I'm heading over to the Burger King. The food here sucks big time!"

"I suppose I'll be seeing more of you soon?" Larissa bit her lower lip.

"Yeah, definitely. Oh, and Stella, I'll be back by ten-fifteen to get you."

"Coolie!" Stella waved as Jason vanished into the clusters of people.

Meanwhile, Larissa couldn't take her eyes off him. There was no point in hiding it––she had fallen for him.

"Now tell the truth, Larissa," Stella had jolted her out of her daze, "have you met my brother before?"

"Stella, what's the big deal if I've met him or not?"

"Nothing, it's just, you acted like you were in love with him or something?"

*You don't know how right you are,* Larissa thought happily.

\*\*\*\*\*\*\*\*

"Hey, party people! Are you having fun?" A voice shouted into the microphone. It was coming down to the wire now, and most of the people were relaxing around the pool. Brittany had made the announcement.

Larissa noticed Brittany wink her eye at Cher, who was sitting at the bar. She got up from her stool and went to stand by Brittany. The whole crowd cheered, except for Stella and Larissa. *What is she doing?* Larissa thought.

Brittany continued, "Well, get ready for more fun as we present to you the main event of the night!"

The girls gave each other strange looks.

Gia, Tara, and Jade pushed through some people to catch up with her friends.

"Hey, watch it, tubby," Tara snarled when one fat guy smacked into her face.

Jade was the first to speak. "What is Brittany doing," she asked.

"Nothing good," Larissa retorted.

"You got that right!" Gia shouted. "Whatever that 'main event' is has trouble written all over it!"

"Hello! Trouble is their middle name!" Tara shouted. The girls giggled after Tara's comment and then continued to hear Brittany, speculating what the dangerous duo was up to now.

"We'll be having a chicken match. It'll be Cher"—she pointed to her as she waved to the crowd like she had just won a beauty pageant—"against one lucky winner!"

The crowd cheered some more and raised their hands up in the air, shouting, "Pick me! Pick me!" Mary Ann, a twelfth grader who was the event coordinator, shuffled the pieces of paper in a basket. She picked up a paper and handed it to Brittany.

"And the winner is . . . Stella Kirkpatrick!" Larissa, Tara, Jade, Gia, and Stella were all surprised to hear Stella's name be called.

"Did you enter the contest," Tara asked her.

Stella shook her head in disagreement. "No way," she shouted. "I didn't even know there was a contest until now!"

Larissa rolled her eyes. *I can't believe they can't figure this one out!* "That's because there was never a contest to begin with!" Larissa said to her friends.

"Then why would they lie and say Stella's the winner?" Gia asked.

"I don't know, but whatever the reason is, it's not going to be pretty!"

"Then what do I—"

But before she could finish her sentence, Cher had caught up with Stella and her friends. "Don't worry, girls," Cher told them. "Stella's in good hands."

"Hardly," snapped Larissa.

"Wow, Larissa," Cher said, "ever since you ditched me for these"—she glared at them up and down—"riff raffs, you've really gotten bold."

Larissa's eyes narrowed. She had waited a long time to say this, and now was the perfect time to say how she felt. "Go rot in hell."

Cher stared at her in silence for a moment. "I'll pretend I didn't hear that." And then, she dragged Stella over to the booth.

When she was gone, Gia shouted out, "Let's follow her!" And so they did.

*Cher has to be doing something terrible!* Larissa thought. *I can feel it!*

The spotlight was shone on Stella as she walked up to the DJ booth. The light burned her eyes, and to make matters worse, those same girls who were gossiping about her before were at it again.

"Her outfit is so fugly," one girl said. "Was she blindfolded when she got dressed?"

"No, I don't think she was blind," her partner-in-crime remarked. "She's just fugly!" She and her friend cackled like wild hyenas.

Stella tried her best not to listen to them.

"So, Stella," Brittany said once Stella was standing across from her, "do you accept my challenge?"

Stella wanted to say no, but Brittany began to whisper into her ear. "If you don't, too bad! You can't wiggle yourself out of this one!"

"Why did you choose me, then?" Stella whispered back.

"We have our reasons!" Cher, who had butted into the conversation, answered. She stepped back out of the conversation to let Brittany finish the job.

Brittany stepped in. "Take the challenge," she commanded. "Between you and me, this might even clean up your reputation. See those girls"––she pointed at the ones who were mocking her––"they're nothing but losers who like to gossip about everyone and everything but themselves. But, if you accept, I can guarantee all this will stop, and Cher and I will leave you alone!"

Stella paused for a moment. "How do I know you aren't lying to me?"

Brittany held out her pinkie. "Because I pinkie swear it!"

Stella glared at her pinkie for some time. Her sharp manicured nail protruded upward towards the heavens. *Well, it's worth a shot.* She locked pinkies with her. "Let's do it!"

Brittany flashed a sly smile at her. "Excellent," she said and tightly squeezed her crossed fingers together. They unlinked their pinkies and turned back to the crowd. "Looks like we have ourselves a competition!"

The crowd hooted and hollered in approval.

********

"She went through with it?" Gia asked in the midst of the excitement.

"I guess she did." Tara sighed. The four girls were now sitting at a table by the pool, waiting for Cher and Stella to come out of the locker room in the bikinis provided by the hotel.

"But why would she," Jade asked. "I mean, doesn't she suspect something's up? It's Cher and Brittany we're talking about!"

"They must've said something to her. Something she wanted!" Larissa said. "There's no way Stella would've agreed to this just like that!" Just then, they spotted Stella and Cher stroll out of the locker room both wearing matching yellow halter-top bikinis. The girls watched as they walked toward the DJ table once more.

Stella and Cher waited by the edge of the pool while Brittany announced something into the microphone again. "Are any guys out there willing to be their bases," she asked. All the guys raised their hands, mainly because they were hoping they would be Cher's base.

Brittany chose Chris and Patrick, an eleventh grader who wasn't popular, but well liked by others. They leaped into the pool and splashed all the guys and girls sitting around it, including Larissa and her friends.

Tara wiped the chlorinated water off her skin. "It would've been easier if he had just walked in like everyone else," she whined. Her friends rolled their eyes. Tara liked to complain about everything!

"Just stop worrying about yourself and worry more about our friend's fate!" Jade suggested. Tara let out a deep sigh and started watching the match again along with her companions.

"Thanks, guys," Brittany acknowledged. "You guys are the best, and might I add looking very hot tonight!"

Some girls whistled and shouted things like, "you got that right" or "take it off".

Brittany handed the mike over to the chubby DJ, who wore an excessive amount of jewelry. "All right. Y'all know the rules—if you fall off your base, you're out!"

"We get it! Just get this stupid thing started!" Cher spat.

"You heard the girl! Let's get it on!" The crowd hollered as the two girls climbed onto the boys' shoulders. Cher was on Chris's shoulders and Stella was on Patrick's.

The fact that she wasn't on her date's base made her jealous, and with Cher on his shoulders instead gave her stomach a lurch.

"You're goin' down, Kirkpatrick," Cher growled.

"Not if I can help it," Stella said back.

"On your mark . . ." The girls sat up straight and braced themselves. "Get set . . ." The girls clasped onto each other's hands and got into position. "Go!" They began to push each other backwards while the crowd screamed and chanted their names.

About five minutes into the game, no one had been knocked down yet. It was proving to be a tough battle. Larissa and the rest of the gang watched them struggling to push each other down.

"Knock her down, Stella!" Gia wailed. "You can take her!" Jade and Tara decided just to holler and clap just like everyone else.

Then there were the occasional 'oohs' and 'aahs'!

Then Larissa noticed something suspicious. Brittany was taking off her sandals and stared at Stella the whole time.

"Guys, look," she whispered to her friends as she pointed at Brittany. The girls gazed over at Brittany. She had just peeled off her cover-up, revealing an emerald-colored bikini and preparing herself to dive in.

"What is Brittany doing?" Tara asked.

"I think she's going to pull Stella's bikini off!" The three girls gasped.

"We have to do something!" Jade shouted. Larissa had to think fast. Then, without hesitating, she quickly sprinted over to Brittany's side.

"Stella, watch ou––" Larissa had twisted her ankle, lost control and fell into the pool. But as she was falling, her hand grabbed something that it was not supposed to.

"Aahhh!" Stella wailed as she dived backwards into the pool.

Cher noticed what had just fallen off of her as well. She jumped off Chris's shoulders and grabbed the item, which was floating around. She snatched it up and climbed out of the pool waving something in her hand. She ran over to the DJ and snatched up the microphone.

Brittany came up to her side "Ladies and gentlemen! We present to you . . ." Cher said. She swung the item over her head like a lasso.

"Stella's bikini top!" Brittany finished.

**Cher and Brittany's plan: completely shallow!**

**Stella being humiliated: too awful to think about.**

Cher threw the top into the crowd, and the guys began fighting over it while the girls laughed hysterically with their friends.

"I knew that would happen or else it wouldn't be considered a chicken match," a blonde girl wearing a cowboy hat and a polka-dotted bikini explained to her friend.

"True."

Larissa had just leaped out of the pool when her friends came over to her with a towel to sop up the water that drenched her body.

"And we owe it all to Larissa!" Cher announced, and the spotlight shone over her soaked body. "Let's give a round of applause to Larissa!" The crowd turned to her and clapped.

"You go, Larissa," one of them shouted out.

"Genius," another said.

Larissa didn't smile; instead she looked at Cher, disgusted by her immoral personality. She wanted to yell out "stop!" but she was too disappointed in herself to do anything. *I don't deserve to be applauded.* She thought sorrowfully. *I deserve to be shot and left for dead!* She hid her eyes from the blinding spotlight. *I'm just more worried about how Stella's handling this. Come to think of it, where is Stella?*

Stella had just pulled on the big T-shirt and pair of ripped shorts she had packed in her colorful beach bag. She was trying to sneak out of the party without being seen, but some ignorant person yelled out, "Look! There she is!"

All the partygoers laughed and pointed at Stella as she raced out of the terrace and down toward the lobby. Her friends noticed her running out of the room as well.

"Stella, wait!" Larissa cried out.

"Hurry! Let's catch up!" Jade ordered. And so they ran out after her with their stuff in tow.

They found her in the lobby, crying uncontrollably.

"Stella, I'm so sorry." Larissa said. But Stella was so mad at Larissa that she smacked Larissa upside her cheek and kicked her in the shin as well.

"Save it," she snapped.

Larissa pressed her hand against her face, cringing in pain. "Stella, I said I was sorry," she pleaded. "I lost my balance and grabbed onto the first thing I could."

"And it just so happened to be my bikini top?"

"She was only trying to help you." Jade spoke up meekly.

Stella fixed her icy stare on her. "Well, she's helped enough," she barked. "Thanks to her, the whole school is in there making fun of me once again!" She pointed at the glass doors leading into the terrace.

They were mostly laughing along with Cher and Brittany, but some looked through the glass and laughed at Stella. One girl even had the nerve to snatch the bikini top from a guy nearby and wave it around. They all looked away in embarrassment.

"See!"

Larissa lowered her head in shame.

"But we were only trying to be good friends and help you out," Gia stated.

Stella scoffed and grabbed her towel, which was sitting on the floor. "Some friends you are!" She glared at all of them before finally saying to them, "See you around. In fact, try not to see me at all!" She stormed out of the lobby just as Jason came walking in.

Rather than being overjoyed to see Jason again, tears traveled down Larissa's face. *I hate myself for being such a klutz! Now Stella won't talk to me, and everyone is going to start congratulating me for something I had no intention of doing!*

"What's wrong with my sister," Jason asked.

"She's just upset about a petty issue. No biggie really." Gia stared down at the parquet floor.

"Don't lie. She only gets that way when something *huge* has happened."

Larissa couldn't stand it any longer. "She's mad at me okay," she forced herself to say. "I slipped and pulled her top off by accident."

"She was only trying to save her though," Jade added. "Brittany and Cher were planning to do that."

"Did you try telling her that?" Jason rattled his keys around.

The girls nodded in accordance. "We tried, but she was so angry she stormed out of here saying we're the worst friends in the world," Gia informed him.

Jason grew quiet for a moment. "What if I try to talk to her on your behalf," he offered. "It's the least I can do to help."

The girls' distressed expressions turned into cheerful ones once they had heard Jason's offer.

"Could you?" Larissa asked.

"I'll try, but I'm not guaranteeing anything!"

"That's cool!" Tara exclaimed. "As long as you try!"

Larissa inched closer to Jason to say something private in his ear while the other girls talked about other ideas to apologize to Stella just in case Jason's idea didn't work. "Do you think you can also tell her I'm truly sorry for embarrassing her, and, if she wants, I still want to be her 'West Coast best friend'?"

Jason nodded. "Sure."

Larissa smiled. "Thanks," she said. "You know, you turned out to be a cool guy, Jason."

"You too . . . wait! I mean a cool—"

Larissa put her finger up to his lips. "You talk too much!" And with that, Larissa finally kissed him.

At first, Jason wasn't sure what to do. Was he supposed to put his hands through her hair or on her hips? But when Larissa placed her hands on the nape of his neck,

Jason figured it was a delicate kiss; not the slobbery ones he was so used to. For the first time in his life, he actually wanted to keep going on and on forever––that is, until…

"Ooh! Jason's got a girlfriend!" The girls chanted.

Larissa and Jason quickly pulled away from each other and wiped their mouths.

"Hey! You shouldn't mock the guy who's pleading to his sister on your behalf!" He said, hoping to change the subject.

"Sorry," Jade said. "Anyway, we'll be waiting for you guys up front."

"And don't keep us waiting," added Tara. "We'd like to leave *tonight*, catch my drift!" The girls began laughing hysterically as they walked over to the seats near the front desk.

Larissa turned to Jason. "So, I guess I'll see you around?"

"Yeah. See you soon." They wanted to give each other a kiss goodbye, but they were afraid the girls would appear out of nowhere and start teasing them again. So instead they gave each other heartfelt hugs.

"Bye," Jason said. He waved to her before he walked down toward the front entrance and out onto the parking lot. Larissa began daydreaming about her kiss. *I'm really starting to like him! Like, honestly, who knew I'd find such a caring (and* cute*) guy right after I dumped that other jerk, Lance!*

That just goes to show how strange love can be sometimes.

But then the horrific thoughts of the bikini flying off and Stella crying flooded back into her mind. *But how can I be happy about my newfound romance when the sister of the guy I like hates my guts?*

And that shows how complicated life is!

Larissa joined her friends over by the front of the lobby to wait for Sam to pick her up. *I just want a hot bath, warm pajamas to slip into, and a good night's rest so I can forget about this whole thing ever happened!* Easier said than done.

## 16

Larissa had just gotten back from her large shopping spree in hopes of forgetting the previous Saturday's unfortunate ordeal. In fact, she committed the whole day to forgetting about Stella and last weekend.

It had been a week since she and her friends had gotten into a fight with Stella, and the road to recovery wasn't that easy. All last week, Stella completely blew her and her friends off. She wouldn't even sit with them at lunch. That's when Larissa knew it was time for some alone-pampering time to clear her mind.

She first got a fresh pedicure and a french manicure at Zen Nail Salon in Mavis Gardens. Next she shopped like crazy on North Rodeo with her daddy's credit card, of course. Then she headed over to the hair salon to get a completely new hairdo, which was why she had brown highlights in her hair and a side-swept bang. And finally, she took Tootsie over to an exclusive pet grooming shop to get her fur spruced up.

Although that had nothing to do with her sadness, she still wanted her dog to feel happy. And when Tootsie was happy, she was happy!

She opened her oversized handbag and let Tootsie jump out. She leaped out of the cramped bag and made a mad dash over to her bed to lie down. She hated that bag! Larissa set her shopping bags down carelessly; knowing Gretchen or Susan would deal with them later. She changed into her light pink terrycloth Juicy Couture tracksuit before grabbing her laptop off her desk and taking it over to her bed. She plopped down on the bed and turned it on.

The screen hummed to life right before her very eyes. When she opened up her instant messaging account, she noticed Tara and Jade were online. She chatted with Jade first:

**Blondie01:** hey Jade!

**WCSweetheart14:** hey Larissa! Still bummed about Stella ☹

**Blondie01:** me 2. What she said about us is still getting me upset. i had 2 pamper myself all day just 2 clear mi mind!

**WCSweetheart14:** yeah. I mean did she have to go so far and call us 'the worst friends in the world?' we were only tryin 2 help

**Blondie01:** no way! She was seriously out of . . . hold on I have another IM coming through.

It was Tara.

**IloveHawaii4life:** am I the only one who is still angry with Stella??????

**Blondie01:** sad, yes: angry, no!

**IloveHawaii4life:** why not? She totally dissed us in our face! Shouldn't we hate her?

**Blondie01:** brb

She switched back to Jade.

**Blondie01:** sorry. Tara was IM-ing me. She's really mad at Stella.

**WCSweetheart14:** tell her Stella has every rite 2be mad at us and we should be mature enough to apologize!

She then went back to Tara.

**Blondie01:** talking to Jade. She said Stella has every rite 2 be mad at us and we should be mature enough to apologize.

**IloveHawaii4life:** yea rite!!!! Stella's my friend and all but she needs 2 know she can't just start yelling at us 4 no reason.

**Blondie01:** but she has a point. We basically embarrassed her in front of the entire school.

**IloveHawaii4life:** But it's not like we planned it that way! Shouldn't she know that?

**Blondie01:** true, but she thinks we did plan it so . . .

**IheartHawaii4life:** well, I'm not apologizing until she learns not 2 accuse her real friends!

IheartHawaii4life has signed off @ 8:02:15 pm

Larissa switched back to Jade.

**Blondie01:** Tara signed off on me cuz she's mad about us not being mad at Stella.

**WCSweetheart14:** *rolls eyes* she's been like that 4 as long as I've known her!

**Blondie01:** do u think she'll . . . hold on. I have another IM.

**WCSweetheart14:** I bet it's Tara back online 2 apologize!

She was wrong.

**DareDevil667:** hey Larissa, it's Jason.

**Blondie01:** how did u get my s/n?

**DareDevil667:** oh yea, don't say hi or anything!

**Blondie01:** im srry. hey Jas. How's it goin? Now can u tell me how u got my s/n

**DareDevil667:** well if it means so much 2 u, i stole it out of Stella's address book . . . rite b4 she crossed it out.

**Blondie01:** *sighs* I'm guessing she REALLY hates us, huh?

**DareDevil667:** I wouldn't put it that way exactly but . . . okay she hates u!

**Blondie01:** *sarcastically* thanks 4 going easy on me!

**DareDevil667:** sorry. Anyway, I was able to dig up some dirt for u!

**Blondie01:** *squeal* tell all!

**DareDevil667:** First of all, she's been up in her room all day...

**Blondie01:** oh no!

**DareDevil667:** what?

**Blondie01:** this is all MY FAULT!!!! If I weren't born a klutz, none of this would've happened!

**DareDevil667:** don't beat urself down like that!

**Blondie01:** how can I not?

**DareDevil667:** well, if u'd let me finish, i overheard her talking 2 some chick named Mariah on the phone?

**Blondie01:** Um...

**DareDevil667:** they were talking about how u guys ruined her chances at becoming popular and proving 2 Cher she isn't a loser . . .? Then i heard 'Homecoming Queen'...

Larissa suddenly let out a gasp. The most brilliant plan came to mind. *That's perfect! The Homecoming dance is coming up this Saturday, and if I come up with the perfect strategy, I can actually have her win this thing! Then she'll prove to Cher she isn't just like the rest of the new kids and she'll be our friend again!*

**Blondie01:** thx Jason! Ur the best!!!!!!

**DareDevil667:** uh . . . thanks?

**Blondie01:** C u l8ter! MUWAH!!!

She ended her conversation with Jason and went back to her conversation with Jade.

**Blondie01:** thanks 4 waiting!

**WCSweetheart14:** no problem. Besides, I have nothing better 2 do here anyway.

**Blondie01:** ROFL!!! Anyway, I was talking 2 Jason

**WCSweetheart14:** OMG!! What did he say?

**Blondie01:** he said Stella's still mad at us but he overheard her saying she wanted to be popular!

**WCSweetheart14:** ur point . . .

**Blondie01:** my point is we make her wishes come true and make her Homecoming queen!!!!!!!!

**WCSweetheart14:** but aren't those results already in?

**Blondie01:** of course . . . which is why I thought about rigging the votes?

**WCSweetheart14:** whoa! Rewind then stop! U WANT US TO RIG THE RESULTS!!!!!!

**Blondie01:** I didn't stutter...

**WCSweetheart14:** do u know how much trouble we'd be in if Principal Carter ever found out WE rigged the election?

**Blondie01:** she won't find out! It's going to be an inside job!

**WCSweetheart14:** And who do u think is going to do that?

**Blondie01:** hold on . . . another IM again. Sorry.

IheartHawaii4life has signed back on @ 8:16:09 pm

**IheartHawaii4life:** hey

**Blondie01:** so u don't entirely hate us?

**IheartHawaii4life:** not anymore, and sorry 4 flipping out on u earlier. Ur rite. We should apologize 2 Stella. Friends?

**Blondie01:** Yeah. Hold on

Blondie01 has invited IheartHawaii4life to a chat room

Blondie01 has invited WCSweetheart14 to a chat
room

WCSweetheart14 has entered

IheartHawaii4life has entered

**IheartHawaii4life:** okay . . . is everyone here?

**Blondie01:** I'm here

**WCSweetheart14:** present! And, Tara, do u 4give
us?

**IheartHawaii4life:** of course. Anyway, what did I
miss while I was gone?

**Blondie01:** Stella is running for Homecoming
queen...@ the last minute...

**IheartHawaii4life:** um . . . haven't the results been
in since last wk?

**WCSweetheart14:** about that, u missed one little
detail––she wants us to rig the votes

**IheartHawaii4life:** cool! I even heard Cher has
been dying 2 be Homecoming queen––even
though she hasn't said much! If we rig the votes
in Stella's favor, Cher would be mortified and
Stella would be our friend again! Perfecto!

**WCSweetheart14:** but aren't u the least bit concerned
about the risks u'd be taking?

**IheartHawaii4life:** duh! But if we don't prove to Cher Stella isn't someone she can torment, who will?

**Blondie01:** at least SOMEONE realizes how significant my plan is!

**WCSweetheart14:** I never said ur plan wasn't great! I just didn't want 2 go 2 jail @ the age of 17!!!!!!

**Blondie01:** 1st, u r not going to jail! I already told u this would be an inside job!

**IheartHawaii4life:** even better!

**Blondie01:** thanks 4 ur support

**WCSweetheart14:** why do I suddenly feel left out?

**Blondie01:** *laughing my butt off*

**IheartHawaii4life:** don't worry. We aren't exiling u or anything.

**Blondie01:** We just want 2 know if u approve of my plan or not? We can't do this without u!

**WCSweetheart14:** why?

**Blondie01:** nope! Can't tell unless u agree!

**WCSweetheart14:** *sighs* fine *thinking*

**WCSweetheart14:** *still thinking*

**WCSweetheart14:** *still thinking*

**IheartHawaii4life:** HURRY UP!!!!

**Blondie01:** I agree!

**WCSweetheart14:** FINE! I approve of ur plan!

**Blondie01:** *screaming inside and out* I can't believe u actually approved!

**WCSweetheart14:** Yeah! Yeah! Yeah! Just clear this up 4 me . . .will I have this put on my permanent record? I have plans for Harvard already in the works!

**Blondie01:** u'll be fine! Trust me

**WCSweetheart14:** ok...so, what's the plan?

**Blondie01:** um . . . I'm still working on that.

**WCSweetheart14:** u mean u haven't thought up a plan yet? AND U WERE BEGGING ME 2 SAY YES????

**IheartHawaii4life:** calm down! All great ideas take time! It didn't take Alexander Graham Bell five minutes to invent the telephone!

**Blondie01:** see . . . Tara doesn't seem to care

**WCSweetheart14:** But Tara doesn't care about anything...no offense, Tara.

**IheartHawaii4life:** No sweat. I prefer to be a free spirit anyway!

**Blondie01:** guys, can we try not to get off task here and think up a plan to get our friend back?

**WCSweetheart14:** okay.

**IheartHawaii4life:** aye, aye, captain!

Larissa began thinking. *We could . . . no!* Tootsie leaped up next to her and began wagging her tail furiously. Larissa held her in her lap and began petting her newly groomed fur. Tootsie was enjoying the pampering, so she lay still as she was showered with strokes. *How does Cher do it? I mean how can she think up these plans, do them and not get caught?*

Then Tara IM-ed her back.

**IheartHawaii4life:** I've got it!

**Blondie01:** TELL US!!!!

**IheartHawaii4life:** Arthur St. Thomas!

**Blondie01:** how is he gonna help us?

**IheartHawaii4life:** well...u c, he has a crush on Jade or whatever, and maybe if Jade can sweet-talk....

**WCSweetheart14:** oh no u don't! That guy freaks me out. He has my picture on his laptop screensaver! Give me an F! Give me an R! Give me an E! Give me an A! Give me a K! What's that spell? —Drum roll—freak!

**IheartHawaii4life:** oh come on, Jade! It's 4 Stella! it's not like u have 2 marry him! It's strictly business, that's it!

**WCSweetheart14:** I know, but does getting our friend back mean jeopardizing my already-ruined social status?

**Blondie01:** but that's what BFF's do! They sacrifice.

**WCSweetheart14:** ugh! if I agree 2 do this, will this be the last time I interact with that sweaty hog!

**Blondie01:** most definitely! This will be the very last time!

**WCSweetheart14:** good. Then I'm in.

**IheartHawaii4life:** YAY!!! I'm so proud of u!!!! *hugs and kisses*

**WCSweetheart14:** *sarcastically* go me!!! But remember, I'm only doing this for Stella!

**Blondie01:** so r we!

**IheartHawaii4life:** now that we're on the same page, can we talk about this plan?

**Blondie01:** sure. And let's hope this is the rite thing...

# 17

It was lunchtime, and instead of eating at Chicke-Dee's and gossiping about the morning's events, Larissa, Tara, Gia, and Jade stood outside the school library, going over last minute details before commencing their plan.

"These heels are giving me a bunion the size of Canada," Jade complained. "How are you able to survive in these things?" She was forced to wear a pair of four-inch kitten heels——courtesy of Larissa's closet——to give her the extra height she desperately needed.

"Would you stop whining and just stay focused?" Larissa exclaimed. She handed her an oversized Jimmy Choo hobo bag. "Take this. These are all the ballots with Stella's name on them."

Jade pouted. "Do I have to do this? I mean, anytime I talk to him, he gets all sweaty and gross-looking!" She tugged at the Rich & Skinny miniskirt Larissa pulled out of her closet for her to wear. "And with this thing on, he'll probably think I'm interested in him!"

"The only reason you're wearing this is because I know you'll get his attention, and when you get his attention, he'll do whatever you want," explained Larissa.

"And what we want is Stella's forgiveness," added Gia.

After pondering on this issue, Jade let out a sigh and said. "Okay, but she's the *only* reason I'm doing this." She turned on her heel and faced the direction of the wood door leading inside. "Wish me luck"––she turned one last time––"but if I get caught, you're all going down with me," she smiled.

Jade began to walk into the library. On her way in, Larissa called out, "We'll meet you at my locker to hear all the details!"

"Okay! See you guys there!" she called out. The girls walked down the hall toward the cafeteria as Jade entered the library where her worst nightmare would be. *He'd better not have skin fungus!* She thought hopefully.

The school library was a two-story room that was decorated to have a 1800s-meets-new-millinium feel. The walls were a simple cream color with cherry columns to accent it. The bookshelves were a lighter color, and they housed thousands and thousands of books covering just about any topic you can think of. The flat-screen desktops were on the opposite side of the entrance.

Jade noticed a bunch of nerdy-looking kids searching for books in the computer technology section. *What a bunch of losers! They use their lunchtime to do this? I can't believe I'm even in here! Wait . . . I'm starting to sound like Cher!* She shuddered. *I hope that never happens again!*

She continued to walk around the large and practically silent library. *Where is he? Isn't this, like, his favorite place in the world? Well, besides the arcade at the mall! Whoa…why do I know that!*

Sure enough, Arthur was sitting at one of the tables, reading a manual on how to use math in certain video games. *You can do this, Jade! You're doing this for Stella!* She held her head up high and ambled up to him as best as she could in the 'stilts' she was wearing.

"What are you reading," she asked when she approached him. He looked up and spotted Jade beside him. He quickly licked his hand and slicked back his curly brown hair. *Ew! Does he really expect me to touch that?* Jade thought in disgust.

"H—H—Hi," He stammered.

Jade spotted some drool dribbling down the corners of his mouth. *He drools too! Does this guy know the definition of hygiene? I mean you'd think since he's a nerd, he'd know these things! Well, I guess I was wrong!*

Jade gulped before speaking to him. "Uh . . . hi, Arthur, long time, no see." *And after this, it'll be a very long time until I see you again! Say when thy kingdom comes!*

Arthur snapped out of his days and started to act normal again. "I'm sorry," he scratched the back of his neck, which was starting to break a sweat. "Did you need anything?"

"Actually, yes, I do."

"Well, whatever it is, I'm your guy!"

A smile swept across her face––the same smile she was so used to seeing the mean girls in the movies using. "Good. Are you handling the votes for homecoming this year, or what I heard was a complete rumor?"

"Yes, I––I mean, yes, I am controlling the votes."

"Well, in that case, can I ask you this one favor?"

"Sure."

Jade leaned in close––but not too close–– to whisper confidential information into his ear. "Can I see the votes before everyone else?"

His eyes nearly burst through his glasses. "That's against the rules! If I reveal those results before the actual homecoming, I can lose that job!"

Jade scoffed. "Oh, come on, Arthur! Live a little! And besides"––she drew little circles on his chest with her pinkie––"it's not like you want to disappoint me, do you?" She couldn't believe how unbelievably Cher-esque she sounded. *There's no way he can turn me down!*

Arthur began hyperventilating again; following some sweat beads forming on his forehead. Jade tried not to cringe when she saw the sweat drops run down his face. *I am so sanitizing when I meet the girls!* "Okay," he tipped closer to her. Jade loathed the feeling of his blazing breath against her skin. *Gross! Get away from me, dragon breath!*

"But you have to promise you won't tell a soul."

She crossed her fingers behind her back. "Cross my heart," she answered. *Anything to get you away from my face!*

"Okay. Follow me." Once he was out of her face, Jade gasped for air as if she hadn't breathed in ages.

He looked back at her with a worried look on his face. "Are you okay?" he asked.

When Jade was able to regain her breath, she answered, "I'm fine!"

"Are you sure?"

"Yeah."

"Do you need to borrow my inhaler?"

*Is this kid for real! I'm not going to use your stupid inhaler after all the problems I've seen you have! First sweating, then drooling then dragon breath! What next? Gingivitis?*

"No, I think I'll be okay."

"Final chance . . ."

*Final chance for what? Death!* "Trust me, I'll be fine."

"Then let's go!" He continued to lead her out of the library. They walked down the hallway until they reached the office. He unlocked the door and led her in. Jade quickly rushed over to the ballot box, which was sitting on a table in the middle of the room. Arthur followed her.

He used a special key to unlock the box. When he opened it, Jade discovered almost all the ballots had Cher's name written on them. She glanced over at Arthur, who was waiting patiently for Jade to be done. *Now how do I get rid of them without Dragon Boy over there seeing?*

"Are you done," he asked.

She turned to Arthur, batting her long, mascara-covered eyelashes. "Arthur, darling," she said in a flirtatious voice, nearly throwing up in her mouth after saying that, "if you wouldn't mind, could you please bring me a wheat shake from Nature's Candy?"

Nature's Candy was the only vegetarian restaurant in the cafeteria. It was put in after the Health Club protested against the unhealthy food choices in the cafeteria's food court. To avoid controversy, the school board decided it would be best to put one in.

"Is that all," he furrowed his bushy eyebrows.

She nodded politely. "Yeah, pretty much."

"Okay, and don't mess around with the votes," he reminded her, wagging his finger in her face. "That would be cheating!"

Jade rolled her eyes. *So what? He's a comedian now! Ha! I'm laughing all over!* "I won't," she flashed him a fake smile.

He grinned back at her and then left the room. As soon as he left, Jade got to work. She had little time to do this, so she didn't waste time. First she locked the door and propped a chair against it. Then she opened the bag and dumped all of Stella's ballots onto the table. Next she grabbed the ballot box and dumped all of the other votes into the purse.

After that she rushed over to the computer, but there seemed to be a problem. *Shoot! I need a password!* She frantically searched through the drawers, but she couldn't find anything. She began punching in random numbers and letters. None of her guesses worked. *Think, Jade! What would be something that would describe Arthur?*

At first, "ratboy "came to mind, but it didn't work. Then she tried her luck with "nerdy16," sixteen being his age. The main screen popped up right before her eyes. *Yes! I figured it out!* Without hesitation, she opened the file with the names of the nominees for homecoming queen inside.

Soon enough, the screen popped up. She read the contents on the page:

**Results for the Cornelius Academy Homecoming Queen:**

Cherisse von Seaton: **550 votes**

Brittany Wellington: **315 votes**

Heather Faulkner: **26 votes**

Maureen Wilson: **9 votes**

Jade reached for the mouse and changed the results so it looked as follows:

### Results for the Homecoming Queen:

Brittany Wellington: **315 votes**

Maureen Wilson: **9 votes**

Stella Kirkpatrick: **550 votes**

Heather Faulkner: **26 votes**

She pressed Save and closed out of the program. She turned off the computer and moved on to the final part of the task. She had rushed over to the ballot box to start stuffing it with Stella's votes and all the rest, purposely leaving out Cher's, when the door began to jingle.

Jade's head shot up in a panic. *That can't be him back so soon!*

"Jade, you in there," he struggled to open the door.

"Uh . . . I'm coming," she called out. She frantically dumped all of Stella's ballots into the box. She could hear some keys ringing on the other side of the door.

"Well, I can't wait! I'm coming in!" At that point she stuffed the remaining part of the ballots into the box. When Arthur opened the door, Jade hastily closed the box and walked up to him.

"Why did you lock the door," he asked once she had approached him.

"I didn't want anyone to know I was in here," she answered informally. "Like you said, you could lose your job."

He let out a chuckle. "Nice work, Agent Jade," he joked.

Jade fought back her laughter. Just for the record, she was laughing *at* him!

"Anyway, I brought you the wheat shake you requested." He handed it to her.

"Thanks. You're a sweetheart," she said.

He stared at her for a moment. "Aren't you going to drink it?"

"Yeah! Just not right now." She peeked over at the clock hanging on the wall across the room. "Anyway, I have to go. Can't be late for class!"

"Oh. I guess I'll see you later," he said to her, disappointed she didn't want to stay longer.

"Sure." She quickly left the room. When she was gone, she chucked the drink into the trashcan. *What a dork! Who drinks wheat shakes anyway?*

She hurried over to Larissa's locker to tell her friends the great news.

**Cher's chances of becoming homecoming queen: null and void! Ha!**

Stella's chances at become popular: good possibility!

# 18

The sun's beaming rays beat down on Larissa's sleepy face. She let out an exhausted moan before arising from her bed and throwing off her cashmere blanket. She checked the time on her alarm clock.

"Eleven thirty," she muttered. She wiped the sleep from her eyes. "I'd better get ready." It was finally the day of the homecoming dance. There was so much pressure riding on this day, she couldn't even handle it. She guessed that's why she woke up so late; the stress was overtaking her life. If everything went well, today would mean she'd made the right choice. But if everything went wrong, this could be the end of all she ever hoped for––to be free from Cher's rule.

She climbed out of her bed and pulled on her cashmere robe. Before she padded into her bathroom, she checked on her puppy. Tootsie was lying on her pink silk pillow, waiting for Larissa to wake up. She was an early riser.

Larissa crouched down and whispered into the dog's bed. "Morning, Tootsie."

Once she saw her owner's face, she quickly leaped off her pillow and began licking her face. Larissa let out a fit of giggles.

"Stop, Tootsie! I have to get ready." Larissa yanked the dog off her face and set her securely on the ground. She stood back up and was heading over to her bathroom when Tootsie began following her.

"I'm sorry, Toots, but you have to wait." Tootsie then put on her sad eyes and began whining.

"Stop it," she scolded. The dog immediately stopped.

Larissa crouched down again to pet Tootsie's fur. She hated to yell at her, but sometimes she had to draw the line. "Don't worry; I'll be done soon." She kissed the top of her dog's head before walking into her bathroom to brush her teeth and wash her face.

********

Susan was in the kitchen cleaning up the table from breakfast. "Morning, Susan," Larissa greeted her maid of three years while she held Tootsie in her arms.

The lanky old woman peered up from her work and grinned. The wrinkles on her cheeks began to squirm up and down. "Good morning, Ms. Evans," she said. "You sure are up late today!"

"I guess I'm stressed about homecoming?" *More stressed than you'll ever know,* Larissa added.

"Don't worry, baby, you'll look gorgeous, as always!"

"Thanks, Susan," Larissa beamed. It seemed she always knew the right things to say.

"Would you like your breakfast now," she asked, busily at work scrubbing a plate in the sink.

"No thanks." Larissa displayed Tootsie to her. "But can you give Tootsie hers?"

"Of course, dear! Your dog will be fed in no time!" She took Tootsie from Larissa's arms and set her on the floor while she got the Pedigree Choice Cuts with Beef dog food from the walk-in pantry.

"Is Mom around?" Larissa called out to her from the kitchen.

"I believe she's out back in her garden right now. I swear she's attached to that patch of land like glue!"

Larissa giggled. "Thanks. I'll be outside if you need me."

"All right, dear!"

The garden was a beautiful oasis of calmness and serenity Deborah had started when they moved into their new home over two years ago. It was her pride and joy—besides Larissa, of course! Larissa found her bent down, watering her petunias and humming a tune cheerfully while she did so.

"I thought we hired gardeners to do this dirty work," she called out.

Deborah turned around and smiled when she saw her daughter. She stood up straight and replied, saying, "We do, but they took the day off."

"Can't daddy fire them?"

"You know your dad isn't like that," she answered. "He specifically told me last night he wanted them to take a break."

"Typical Dad!" They giggled.

When they calmed down, Deborah spoke up again. "Don't you have to get ready for the dance?"

"Yeah, but I need to talk to you first. You know woman-to-woman stuff."

"Sure. We can sit near the fish pond." Deborah led Larissa to the other side of the garden.

They stopped at a white lawn table with two lawn chairs sitting on both sides of it. A green umbrella was hovering overhead to shade them from the early-morning sun. Deborah strolled up to the table to prepare two glasses of lemonade for them.

Larissa, on the other hand, went to feed the fish their breakfast. She grabbed the fish food off the rock it sat on and shook some of the flakes into the pond. Most of the other fish were frightened and swarmed to the opposite side of the pond, but the tiniest fish she chose to call Small Fry stayed to eat. She also fed the other fish their breakfast even if they were still mortified. Once she was done, she walked back over to the lawn table.

Her mother had set out two cups of lemonade and was sitting at the table, waiting for her patiently.

"Thanks," Larissa said after she set her drink down and swallowed it.

"You're welcome." She looked at her daughter worriedly. "So what's wrong?"

Larissa let out a sigh. It had just occurred to her that this was the very first time she had let this much information about her life leave the security of her thoughts.

"Lissa?"

"It's Cher, mom."

"Cher? What happened?"

Larissa took a deep breath and began. "There's this new girl at school, and I began talking to her. She seemed really cool, so we became friends. Best friends, even!"

Deborah's laser-whitened teeth gleamed like the sun when she smiled. "That's great news, honey!"

"Yeah, but . . ." She paused.

"But what," her mom demanded.

She remained silent.

"Larissa, are you all right?" Deborah asked, holding out her drink for her.

She managed to nod her head. "I'm fine. Sorry about that."

"It's okay. Now what were you telling me before your little . . . episode?"

"I was trying to say Cher was starting to get jealous because I started hanging out with Stella a lot more."

"Did you try to make things right with her by including her?"

"No. Cher hated Stella so much, she had to stoop so low by pulling Stella's bikini top off at that party I went to last Saturday."

"That was a mean thing for Cher to even think about!"

Larissa snorted. *I'm guessing she hasn't met the* real *Cher! Not that fake one she acts like in front of grown-ups!*

"Is Stella all right?" Deb asked.

"Well, not exactly. When I was trying to stop Brittany, Cher's new best friend, from pulling the top off, I slipped and pulled her top off . . . but it was an accident, I swear!"

"Did you apologize?"

"I tried, but it didn't work."

"And so what happened next?"

"The right thing! We got back at Cher for hurting her!"

Debbie was so shocked she began screaming at Larissa. "Larissa Kate, haven't I taught you not to seek revenge on others?"

"I know, but I was so angry at Cher. Plus, Stella's my friend, and it's hard for me to see her get hurt like that."

Mrs. Evans's face softened a bit. "That's nice you don't want to see Stella get hurt, but that doesn't mean you have to get even with Cher. Remember, Cher has been your friend longer than Stella has."

Larissa scoffed. "She hasn't been acting like a friend for the past, oh I'll say, three years! All she ever does is push me around!"

"How?"

"She forces me to do whatever *she* wants me to do; not what *I* want!"

Deborah let out a sigh. "Well, this has come as a surprise to me," she paused. "Maybe something happened in Cher's family. You know . . . besides her mother's issues."

Larissa shrugged. "Probably."

"She might even need someone to talk to."

Larissa scoffed. "Don't look at me! I'm through with her! If she needs to talk to me, let her come. She knows where I live!" She sat back in her seat and glanced around the garden, pretending she hadn't heard a thing her mom had said.

When she glanced back at her mother, she noticed her eyes were darted in her direction. "Why are you looking at me?"

"Because, Larissa, Cher needs to talk to you!"

"Me! Why me? Haven't you been listening to me this whole time? I hate her, and, thankfully, she hates me! She won't even look my way anymore!"

"Because she's hurt. Didn't you suddenly ditch her for Stella?"

Larissa slowly nodded her head. "Yes."

"And haven't you been on Stella's side the whole time this 'battle' has been raging on?"

Again, she nodded her head.

*Don't you hate it when moms are right?*

"Larissa, listen to me. Cher is your best friend. You guys may fight and hate each other for some time, but remember . . . she'll always be there for you no matter what."

"Yeah right! Whoever made up that line hasn't met the Cher I know!"

"Larissa, just take my advice and talk to her. You never know when she might surprise you."

Larissa thought for a moment. *I'm not sure how this plan will work out, but . . . I trust Mom's advice. If she says it will work, it will work!*

"Thanks, Mom." She got up from her seat and hugged her.

"You're welcome," she stated after they pulled away from each other. "Are you going to get ready now?"

"Yeah. I'm heading over to the salon with Jade and Tara to get some highlights and possibly a haircut."

"Jade and Tara? Who are they?"

"Also some new friends of mine."

"Oh! Well, have fun, and don't be coming back with some wacky hairstyle that will give me a heart attack!"

Larissa laughed. "I won't." She was about to leave the outdoor garden when her mother spoke again.

"Oh, and remember, your curfew is midnight." Larissa rolled her eyes, but in a good way. She was used to her mom's strict curfews. That's just how her mother was.

"I'll be home by then," she groaned.

"Okay. See you."

"Bye." She headed back to her room to take a shower and change into some regular clothes. After that, she logged on to her IM account to see if the girls were on.

Tara was signed on.

**Blondie01:** Hey Tara! Just about ready 2 head over 2 the salon?

**IheartHawaii4life:** totally! I'm so stoked! Jade is over my house rite now. Gia's coming over after she buys a dress!

**Blondie01:** lol!!! Can't believe it took her this long 2 buy a dress?

**IheartHawaii4life:** me 2. anyway, c u in a bit.

**Blondie01:** c ya!!!!

Blondie01 has signed off @ 12:08:46 pm

She grabbed the sky blue Alberto Makali chiffon party dress off the rack, still safely wrapped inside the dry cleaner plastic, a pair of Prada evening pumps, gathered some accessories, and left her estate with high anticipations for tonight.

# 19

The dance had just gotten started, and the rooftop of the exclusive Chaney Hotel was already getting crazy! Everyone was dancing to Nelly's hit song "Hot in Herre," which was being blasted through the huge speakers.

Brittany and Cher walked in and noticed all the people dancing and having a good time. Of course, the room would suddenly stop and stare when Cher graced into the room. Such things always happened when she made a grand entrance.

After a long battle with her personal stylist that morning, Cher settled on a tight-fitting Mandalay beaded cocktail dress, which according to her said, *"I didn't try hard to put together this outfit, but I know I look good,"* with a pair of Michael Kors Candi sandal heels. With her hair up in a serious, yet flirty, bun gave her outfit the perfect touch of sophistication.

"This dance is off the hook," Brittany squealed above the music. She chose to wear a black Yoana Baraschi sateen dress that hugged her beloved curves flawlessly and jeweled-encrusted Miu Miu T-strap heels.

"Duh, otherwise, we wouldn't be here!" She then gazed over at Brittany with a smirk across her face. "Ready to show off our dresses to all those losers who were left to shop at Sears?"

Brittany let out a giggle. "Born ready!"

"Then let's go find 'em!" The girls strutted over to the refreshment table, their first stop.

********

"Who do you think is going to be homecoming queen?" Janette asked.

Janette was considered rich even though her father inherited her grandfather's wealth. She grabbed a piece of american cheese on a toothpick and plopped it into her mouth.

"My guess: Cher, as always," her friend Alicia answered.

Alicia's family was equally as rich as Janette's. Her father was a movie director for Opaque Film Productions. Her mother was an actress for major motion movies and small roles on TV sitcoms.

Alicia threw her napkin and toothpick into the garbage can nearby. At that point Cher and Brittany arrived at the table, intimidating most––if not all––of the losers who couldn't find people to dance with. The girls brushed right past the two girls without even a simple greeting being offered.

Cher picked up a piece of broccoli from the veggie tray and dipped it into the dressing in the middle. But instead of eating it, she stared at it blankly.

"You don't think this dressing has that many calories in it, do you," she asked Brittany.

Brittany was pouring herself a glass of sparkling cider. "I doubt it." She took a sip of her drink. "I mean, who would put fattening dressing near *vegetables*?" The girls laughed at the thought.

Janette and Alicia were hoping Cher would greet them, but the way her conversation was going, it wasn't her main priority.

"Why didn't she say hi to us?" Alicia whispered.

Janette shrugged and bit into another cube of cheese. "Maybe she didn't see us?"

"Of course she did," she whispered loudly. "Didn't you see the dirty look she gave us when she was approaching the table?"

"No," she said with her mouth full.

"That explains it!"

Alicia wiped around her mouth with a napkin. "Well, I'm going to say hi."

"Leesha, no! What if she's not in the mood to talk to us?"

"Then I'll make her be in the mood!"

She threw her napkin away before she confidently walked up to Cher and Brittany. "Hey, Cher," Alicia said happily.

Cher and Brittany spun away from the table. They shot her a disgusted look once they saw her. "Uh . . . do I know you," Cher scoffed.

Alicia tried her best not to break down in front of Cher. If not, she'd be marked for mimicking the rest of her life. "I'm Alicia." Cher was still looking at her strangely.

"And why should I care?"

Her hands began to shake. "I'm in your PE class, remember?"

"Oh. You're the one who lost her pants after class that one day, right?" Brittany burst out laughing while Alicia stood there, blushing. She had lost her pants one time after gym class, but that was only because someone had hidden them in the garbage can.

"Yeah, that's me."

Brittany calmed down from her laughter. "So, did you ever find those rags?"

"Yeah," Alicia nervously laughed. "They were stuffed in a trashcan."

"That could be a sign they belonged there," Brittany added eyeballing a biscotti.

Cher let out a loud yawn, indicating she was bored with the conversation and that it had better change soon! "Anyway, what did you want from us," she asked impatiently.

"I was wondering . . . are you nervous about the homecoming queen results?"

"Psh, no! I know I'm going to win! There's no way I can't! I mean look around," Alicia obeyed, "where's the competition?"

"O-oh, well, I hope you win!"

"I know! But it's okay. I'll just pretend I care."

"See you later." She muttered, and she walked back with Janette in shame.

Once she was out of earshot, Cher and Brittany almost immediately started gossiping. "Did you see her dress?" Cher asked.

"You mean that potato sack she was wearing was supposed to be a dress?"

The girls burst out laughing. "And her hair! Two words: bird's nest!"

"And what was she thinking coming over here with her dorky best friend trying to talk to us in the first place?"

"Trying to be your BFF, like every other loser at this dance!"

"True."

There was a silence between the two for a moment.

"Do you want to hit the dance floor?" Brittany asked after a moment. She pointed down at her silver crystal Miu Miu T-strap heels. "I paid seven hundred and ten dollars for these, and they are *not* going to waste just standing around!"

"You go ahead. I'm just going to stay here for a while and freshen up a bit."

"Suit yourself." Brittany sauntered over to one of the tables where Clyde and his preppy guy friends were sitting. They talked until Clyde led her out to the dance floor by the hand. *I always suspected she had a major crush on him!* Cher thought as she watched Brittany and Clyde sway to Akon's song "Don't Matter." *Now if only I could find a guy like him…if only Stella didn't take him away from me…*

Larissa, Jade, Tara, and Gia arrived around nine fifteen after a delay at the salon. (I mean, you'd think these people would know the difference between curls and waves)! The girls left their handbags and clutches at the coat check before entering the dark room.

"Thnks fr th Mmrs" by Fall Out Boy was now blaring through the speakers. Tara bobbed her head to the music, not minding the fact her hair was probably flying all over the place now. "I love this song," she exclaimed.

Gia, who was also dancing, shouted, "Me too!"

"Guys, focus!" Larissa shouted.

The girls almost immediately stopped dancing.

281

"What's up?" Jade asked.

"I'm still worried about this plan," she said. "Do you think it worked?"

"Yeah," hollered Jade. "It was totally the best plan ever!"

"Weren't you the same one telling us this plan had some serious consequences?" Tara mocked.

Jade rolled her eyes. "Well, I was wrong! There!"

"Aha! So you finally admit you were wrong!" Larissa exclaimed.

She blushed. "Yes, now can we stop worrying about this election and go dance?"

"She's guilty," said Gia

"You guys . . ."

"Okay, sorry." Tara said.

"Thank you! Now let's go get our groove on!" She led the way to the center of the ballroom and began dancing to the music despite all the wandering eyes judging them.

Cher grabbed a strawberry from a bowl, dipped it into the chocolate fountain, and ate it whole. They were just about to announce the homecoming king and queen, and she was starting to feel nervous. *I know I'm going to totally win! I always win! That's how it's been for two years . . . and it's about to become three!* Then she clutched her stomach as if she was about to hurl. *So why do I have this funny feeling I might not get my title?*

Cher quivered at the thought of losing. *That's my spot! I'm the only one who can be wearing that tiara! Not some wannabe! I'm going to wear that crown and I am going to parade around the room, saying,* "You wish you were me!" *to everyone . . . and no one can take that away from me. No one.*

Stella arrived at the hotel just around the same time Principal Carter was about to announce the homecoming king and queen. She had her dad drop her off late so no one showing up in expensive cars and limos would start insulting her dad's station wagon or start bringing up last Saturday. She hadn't told her parents because she knew they'd just tell the principal and make a big scene about it. That would be a pass for everyone at school to make fun of her even worse than they already did!

"Excuse me, students," she heard Principal Carter call out. The students gave her their attention. She was standing on a makeshift stage with vice principal Yamaguchi. The DJ turned down the music so they could listen.

"It is now time to announce your choice for this year's homecoming king and queen!" The students cheered.

Principal Carter signaled for them to quiet down. She pulled out an envelope and ripped it open. "And your choice for homecoming king is . . . Mr. Brian Connors!"

Brian walked up onstage as his friends high-fived him. He was popular and amazingly cute. His body was toned from playing on the soccer team with Tommy in the spring and ice hockey in the winter. He was also notorious for being somewhat of a loner.

Stella couldn't help but stare at him. *He's the most gorgeous creature to walk the earth,* she exclaimed in her mind. She walked closer to the stage just to get a better glimpse of his face. *It would be so cool if I could win . . .*

"And your choice for Homecoming queen is. . ."

Brittany turned to Cher. "Are you ready to win this thing," she asked.

"Of course!"

Meanwhile, Larissa was standing on the opposite side of the gym and turned to her friends. "Ready to get our friend back," she asked them.

"Totally!" Tara answered for them.

Principal Carter ripped open the envelope. At that point, it felt like time was slowing down. Both Cher and Larissa anxiously waited for the results.

Carter held the piece of paper high and said, "Ms. Stella Kirkpatrick!" The crowd hollered, although some were confused.

Stella's mouth opened wide in shock. *I can't believe it! I won! But who would vote for me?*

Take a wild guess.

After vice principal Yamaguchi put the Swarovski-crystal tiara on her head, Stella walked over to her throne next to Brian while the photographers took their picture.

Brian moved closer to her. "You look really pretty tonight," he complimented.

Stella blushed as she fixed her red and black corset. "Thanks," she whispered back. She smiled as another picture was taken. She turned back to Brian.

"So how does it feel to be my queen," he joked.

Stella giggled. "I feel very lucky."

Brian paused and gazed deeply into her eyes. "Me too."

Stella's cheeks reddened after that flattering comment. *I'm really starting to like this guy! Like* really *like him. Maybe it's love at first sight?*

Brian continued. "So I was wondering if you'd li––"

Principal Carter interrupted him, and Stella cursed her for that. She just knew he was asking her on a date. "And now your homecoming king and queen will share their first dance together."

*Now that I like!* Stella exclaimed in her thoughts.

"You are allowed to dance around them if you'd like, but remember to give them the necessary space."

The DJ turned the music back on. A popular rock song blared through the speakers. Brian and Stella began dancing onstage, and everyone started to join them.

"Great job, Stella," one guy congratulated.

She was shocked. *People are actually congratulating me?*

"You look so hot!" Sanjiv Malacca, an Indian exchange student, commented. He was known around school to be a pervert. *And flirting?*

"Uh . . . thanks?" she blushed.

Sanjiv winked and was about to kiss her hand, but Brian put a stop to it.

"Hey, man! Back off!"

*He's so protective of me!* Stella exclaimed in her mind. *I wonder if he likes me.* But then a thought came back to Stella's mind. *Who would vote for me? I mean, I thought I was dubbed a loser around here. Unless . . .* She spotted her target sitting at a table, sulking. She turned back to Brian and spoke softly into his ear.

"I'll be right back." He smiled at her when she pulled away from his ear.

Stella made her way off the stage and headed over to her friends. *It's time I make things right!*

********

Larissa and her friends were sitting at a table in a lonely corner, wondering if their plan to make Stella their friend worked.

"Do you think she knows it's us?" Tara asked.

"I hope!" Jade answered back. "I would hate to see all my hard work of flirting with that disgusting pig go to waste!"

"Jade!" They all shouted.

"What? I'm only speaking the truth."

"Can you, for once in your life, be a bit considerate?" Gia begged.

Jade sighed. "I'm sorry."

Larissa let out a deep sigh. "I just hope she'll be our friend again."

"Yeah." Her friends said in unison.

Suddenly, they heard a voice call out to them. "Is there room for one more," the person inquired. The girls looked over at the person standing there and discovered it was Stella!

"Sure," Gia responded happily. "Pull up a chair." Stella pulled out a chair in between Tara and Larissa and sat down. There was an awkward silence between the girls.

"So," Jade said, "how have you been?"

"Pretty good," Stella answered. Then they went back to being silent.

Larissa was getting tired of the irregular behavior. And if they weren't going to say it, she would. "Stella, I am *so* sorry for pulling your bikini top off!"

Stella froze and stared at her for a while. "Wow. I didn't think you cared that much anymore."

"We do care, Stella!" Jade announced. "You're our best friend!"

Stella couldn't help but feel a little remorseful towards them. *Maybe they do care? What am I saying? Of course they care!* She quickly shot up from her seat and hugged Jade. "I'm sorry I didn't believe you guys before." Tears began dripping down her cheeks. "I should've believed you in the first place."

********

"Don't worry about it," Larissa said. "We forgive you." And when she said those words, a sudden sense of relief fell over her. And that's all the feeling she needed. Her plan had worked after all—tonight would go down in history as the best night of their lives.

********

"Thanks," Cher grumbled to the poor ninth grader working the coat check. "Oh, and next time you wear shorts, you might want to shave your legs." She pointed out her hairy thighs to the girl. She hated to be so rude, but she had to take her anger out on someone.

Cher stomped out of the ballroom with Brittany close to her side, not even caring the girl was turning bright red. "I can't believe she won," she wailed. "I mean, what does she have that I don't?"

Brittany opened her mouth to say something, but Cher beat her to it. "Nothing, exactly!"

"Cher, don't worry about it," Brittany assured her. "By Monday, everyone will forget she won!"

"Yeah, but—"

But then, she overheard Larissa and the surfer chicks giggling over by coat check. She had heard they decided to head down to the pizza shop and then over to Stella's house to catch up and hang out just like old times.

Brittany was confused as to why Cher suddenly stopped speaking. "Why did you—" Cher put up her hand and shushed Brittany so she could hear the girls talk.

"Well, I'm leaving you here!" Brittany turned on her heel and walked outside to wait for Richmond to come pick her and Cher up.

"So, you were just trying to help me?" Stella asked Larissa.

"Yeah," Larissa answered. "I saw Brittany about to jump in, so I had to do something!"

"Well, thanks."

Jade cut into the conversation, but first looked around to make sure nobody could hear them. Cher was hidden behind a fake palm tree, well out of sight.

"I guess this is a good time to say we rigged the results for the show so that you could win homecoming queen."

That was all Cher had to hear.

She couldn't believe it! *So they set this up? I can't believe my own best friend would do this to me! She knew how much being homecoming queen meant to my popularity, but she took it away from me because of Stella! That witch! Well, she won't get away with this! She hasn't seen the last of me . . .*

Stella eyes beamed with joy. "I can't believe you guys would do that, just for me," she exclaimed, surprised yet happy about what her friends had done for her. "What made you do it?"

"Well, we got some info from your brother," Tara informed her. "He told us you wanted to be popular, so we decided being homecoming queen would help."

Stella rolled her eyes. "He can never keep a secret," the girls laughed, "but I'm glad he told you guys." She choked back some more tears. "You didn't have to do this."

"We're friends! It's what we do!" Jade said.

"So, are we friends?" Larissa asked, staring hopefully in Stella's direction.

Stella smiled at her, knowing exactly what she'd say next. "Now and forever!"

They were finally friends . . . for now.

\*\*\*\*\*\*\*\*

"This school must be buying crack from her because there is no way she could've won!" Brittany exclaimed once Cher came out to meet her on the sidewalk. "What could they possibly see in her?"

Cher squeezed her clutch tightly. Her fingertips turned pale white. "Nothing!"

"What are you talking about? She won homecoming queen!"

"And now I know why!"

"What do you mean?"

"Larissa and her homo friends set this up. They changed the results so Stella could win, not me!"

Brittany dropped the jaw of her glossed mouth. "No way," she exclaimed. "I can't believe they'd do that! Can't they get expelled or something?"

"Of course, but they didn't get caught! It must've been an inside job!"

"With who?"

Cher had to think for a moment. "I don't know, but I'm going to find out!"

"So what are you going to do about it until then?"

Cher grinned slyly at her. "Sit back and wait."

Printed in the United States
129576LV00001B/28-36/P